CURSED

NEW YORK TIMES BESTSELLING AUTHOR
SHAWNTELLE MADISON

A Collection of Coveted Short Stories

A CRAVING LIKE NO OTHER

CHAPTER 1

THE UNIVERSITY OF PITTSBURGH campus was dead. Not that there were zombies lurking about, but Pitt tended to have a few students who looked undead during midterms. Spring break had hit earlier this week and now Pitt had quieted a bit. After the weekend ended, everything would be business as usual.

Right now I lugged a suitcase and backpack across campus to meet my ride for a weekend of fun. As to why he didn't just meet me outside of my dorm was another story. He'd sent me a brief text message not too long ago: *Meet me outside of the Chevron Science Center. If you don't show up, I'll still make you come.*

I snorted even though a delicious shiver went down my spine.

I'll still make you come.

I'd only known Thorn Grantham for a few months, yet

just thinking about him tossed my mind headfirst into the gutter.

I hit a bump in the sidewalk, and my black luggage teetered a bit. The honeyed feeling left quickly as I tried to reach my destination.

I'd tied my hair back, but a wind had pulled several light brown strands into my face. They got into my mouth often enough to frustrate me to no end.

"Son of a bitch." By the time I reached the Chevron Science Center, I was ready to perform evil science experiments on Thorn for making me haul my stuff this far. And the science center was a perfect place to dish up a chemical cocktail or two.

A black Ford Explorer was parked in the nearby car lot. Even though it was running, I wondered if it was his, until I spotted a tall blond man waiting outside. The wind blew toward me, and there was no mistaking I'd found him.

He leaned against the truck, watching the cloudy sky. Spring had arrived, but the bleak weather still lingered. Just looking at him sparked every nerve in my stomach. He was beautiful to behold.

"What took you so long?" he grumbled. Then he looked at my suitcase and bag and frowned.

"If you would've picked me up at Langley you wouldn't have waited so long."

He grunted. "First of all, I had to turn in a report. Second, don't think we're heading into the woods with your super suitcase there."

I patted my bag, which might've looked a bit bulky, but everything I needed to feel comfortable was inside. "It's just a few things."

"You won't need *all* that."

"How do you know what's in there? Your vision isn't as good as Superman's."

Thorn opened the back of the SUV, then he waited with his arms crossed. Did he want me to take a peek inside? I checked and couldn't miss the obvious: only a single camping backpack was there. Apparently, he'd left his life behind in his apartment.

"I don't need x-ray vision to know you packed half of Pittsburgh in there," he said. "Was there a few students who didn't have a place to go and you threw them in there as snacks?"

I sneered for good measure. "It's my chemistry professor if you really want to know."

Thorn smiled and I about melted. "Yeah. I would've packed him, too."

He took my suitcase and tossed it in the back. When I watched the way his jeans hugged his ass, I was just a little bit ashamed. His gray T-shirt molded over his chest and offered the best view I've had all day.

I looked at my clothes. Thank goodness, I had a pair of jeans to wear or I would've looked out of place. Normally I'm set in my ways when it comes to clothes. I like things in a certain manner. The placement of my suitcase was one of them. After Thorn went around to the side of the car, I added my backpack and turned my suitcase so it lined up properly with my backpack and his. I could've left it alone, hell things might get jostled on the way to the park, but at least I'd worry less about it.

Then I reached for my suitcase again.

"Let's go, Natalya!"

I slammed the back shut and hurried to the front. He seemed to get a lot bossier when he was around me. Not that I minded it. It was more of a "push" as we werewolves would call it. A gentle bite on the scruff of the neck. I liked it.

"Keep moving, woman. Daylight is running out." He grinned.

"You cleaned out your truck," I said.

The seat was free from fast food bags and candy bar wrappers. Thorn had a sweet tooth and did little to curb it. When I'd first rode in his truck a few weeks ago, I'd been horrified. Not that it was nasty or anything—I'd seen worst in most of the dorm rooms near mine.

Now that he'd recently washed and vacuumed everything out, the car smelled nice.

Had he done that for me?

"There wasn't much." He kept his eyes on the road as we left campus. I did the same, but I still squirmed a bit.

"How long until we get there? I wish you would've told me where we're going."

He chucked. "And spoil the fun?"

I groaned. "Just because I planned out our study date doesn't mean I'm that way all the time."

"I didn't mind it. At first. But when we had exactly thirty minutes per subject, and I had to drink that god-awful tea, I thought you were pushing things a teeny bit too far."

"Green tea is good for studying, and based on your attention span, you have me to thank for completing all of your assignments that night."

Less than a foot separated us while we spoke. His hand lingered on the armrest just a few inches from my leg. The fingers twitched twice and naturally my imagination drifted to the wrong place. He had such long fingers. Thick forearms that flexed as the fingers moved. What would those hands feel like on me?

"I did get everything done," he said, hopefully unaware

of my thoughts. "But you need to loosen up. We could've had more fun."

My heart sank. "You were bored?"

"Not in the way you think. There's nothing wrong with sitting next to a pretty lady in a quiet study room."

My mouth went dry and I broke my gaze away from his hands.

I wasn't sure what to say. He was often a man of few words when we were alone.

Eventually, we left campus and Thorn drove us northeast on I-80. I still had no idea where he planned to take us. There were a few state parks north of us—they were ideal places for werewolves to run during the full moon. Not that I had done research. I was too busy completing homework due after spring break. A few teachers had given me assignments. Didn't they expect most of the students to relax and waste perfectly valuable time? Perhaps sit around on beaches drinking fruity drinks? Since it was my first year at Pitt, I'd never had the spring break college experience. Until Thorn had poked me to go with him I'd planned to go home and hang out with my parents in Jersey.

"Are we going back to South Toms River?" I asked.

"Nope."

I guess I would have to wait. The city of Pittsburgh slowly disappeared and turned into the countryside. Trees surrounded the highway. I rolled down the window and inhaled. There were so many wonderful scents: small birds, rabbits, maple trees, and even pine. The wolf within me twitched in excitement. Small game hid nearby. They lurked among the trees.

Thorn turned on the radio and oldies rock music blasted through the speakers. I hummed along to Credence Clearwater's *Bad Moon Rising*.

He actually liked mellow music, which surprised me. When I first met him I thought he'd be one of those types who liked grunge or hard rock, but when he picked me up to take me to the coffee shop for our first date, I'd learned he loved jazz music—just like me.

"There's just something about the rhythm and beat in those days," he'd said to me at the time. *"It gets under your skin and it stays there. I do a lot of thinking by myself and that's the music I listen to."*

Less than an hour into the ride we approached the turnoff for the first state park. I looked at him, but he said gruffly, "Not good enough."

He practically had a reply for every park we passed for the next two hours. "I wouldn't run in that place if you strapped a rabbit on my back and told me to run."

"Then what is good enough? We're only an hour or two from New York?"

"You'll see. Don't you have any patience?"

"When I'm kept in suspense, I don't."

Four hours into the drive and the landscape had changed. We'd traveled for a while east and now the terrain was full of rolling hills covered with trees. We passed so many state parks—until we made the turn to go south on Highway 594. A straight shot to Hickory Run State Park.

"About time we got somewhere," I said.

Thorn merely chuckled.

It was all he'd promised. The park entrance drew us in with welcome arms, but there were other scents here that seemed familiar. Other werewolves had been here. At least twenty-four hours ago.

Thorn parked the SUV in a nearby visitor parking lot. From a few spots down, a man strolled up to our car. Based on his scent—a sour sweaty musk—he was a werewolf who hadn't been around other werewolves a lot. He was a rogue without a pack. He was also much smaller than Thorn, but he had a friendly enough smile. He tapped the driver's side window to get our attention, and Thorn rolled his window down.

The stranger kept his gaze on the ground as he addressed Thorn. "Saw you two come in and I thought I'd warn you."

"Is something wrong?" Thorn asked.

The man only wore a dirty blue T-shirt and jeans. His eyes were quite small for such a round face. I was surprised to find someone with such a strong scent—a raw fear that indicated he'd rank even lower than me in my pack.

"I'm supposed to ward off others. The local Pine Bluff Pack has closed off the western part of the park to rogues."

We had entered the park from the west. So that was why the entrance smelled so strong. Another pack had marked the territory here. Their calling card practically yelled, *"Piss off."*

"I'll take that under advisement," Thorn said without blinking. "Thanks."

The man backed away from the car. "No problem."

Thorn didn't say anything for a bit. He merely scanned the parking lot. Almost as if somebody would just pop up and force us to leave. I looked out the window and wondered what he saw, but he merely shrugged.

Maybe he thought we weren't in immediate danger.

Thorn turned off the car and left the SUV. I slowly followed. Other families around us took out gear for fishing or camping. We weren't the only one with plans.

Thorn unloaded his backpack.

"We're staying?" I asked.

"Yep. "

"But that guy said—"

"He said there are rogues." Thorn was calm. I wish I knew why. "No biggie. We'll stay out of their way. Rogues don't travel in large groups."

"Why don't we hang out with humans on the campgrounds?" I asked.

"I doubt the humans would want us nearby when the full moon comes."

He did have a point there, so I nodded.

I reached for my suitcase, but Thorn closed in and placed his hand on it.

"No?" I whispered. I couldn't look at his face, but I could smell his intentions. I wasn't getting my way.

"No," he said with a hint of amusement in his voice.

Thorn would be an alpha someday. Sensing it was easy. The need to cower or avert my eyes was second nature around him.

"What if I need something in there?" My voice had grown quiet.

"I'll take care of you."

"Flashlights? A tent? Cooking supplies?"

"All covered."

Now that comment scratched my hide the wrong way. Did he really think his measly backpack had all that?

This time I did look him in the eye. Only to find him looking right back at me. I swallowed deeply and inhaled. His arousal was as strong as mine. In the past we'd sat next to each other. Studied next to each other. But it was almost as if a line was waiting to be crossed before our relationship would change.

One of us would cross the boundary sooner or later.

He leaned toward me, his free hand gripping my arm. Gently he pulled me away from the suitcase. Or should I say, he pulled me closer to him. His mouth brushed against my ear, eliciting a shiver that ran a path of fire down my stomach to my core.

"I'll take care of you," he insisted.

I sighed. He could've taken out a box of toothpicks as supplies and I would've said, "Sounds good to me."

With no place to go, my hand fell to his chest. Perhaps I'd put it there to add space between us, but it did little good. We were body-to-body and I felt everything. His rapid heartbeat. The tight muscles under his shirt. Hell, the raging erection in his pants.

What the hell was I doing? I added some space between us. This was supposed to be a trip where I'd feel safe and less anxious during the full moon. Wouldn't the forest accomplish that goal? Messing around with Thorn shouldn't be part of the plan.

"How about I take what I absolutely need and put it in the backpack?" I suggested.

"Sounds reasonable." He hadn't moved an inch. His expression practically made me want to kick him right then and there.

He knew I wanted him, but would it make a difference that I'd never been with a man before?

While I rummaged through the suitcase, taking out and sorting what I could, I resisted looking over my shoulder at Thorn. He probably found me amusing. I'd seen the way girls looked at him back on campus. He was considered a loner. The kind of man women wanted for a good time. They were all beautiful, outspoken, and popular. Unfortunately none of those adjectives described me.

"We heading out sometime today?" he asked with a chuckle.

His words were a stark reminder I'd stared at a bottle of sanitizer too long. An industrial-sized one at that. I'd live with the travel-sized bottle and some sanitary wipes. I added a few snacks, eating utensils, and another set of clothes to the backpack. They'd have to make do for now.

I turned around twice to rethink my decision, but Thorn took my hand.

"Let's go." He shut the rear door and tugged me toward a path into the forest.

When I glanced back, I couldn't see his vehicle anymore. There was no turning back.

WE'D WALKED for two hours through dense vegetation. My smile never left my face the whole time. Thorn took the led at first, heading due west.

"I love this part of the park," he remarked. "Just north of here is Fourth Run. If we had a canoe, I'd take you for a ride."

"Sounds like fun."

I wished I would've been able to explore more beyond my home state, but my parents didn't travel a lot. Living in a small township was like that.

"Did you come here before with family or with friends?" I asked as we walked between thickets of trees with spring wild flowers growing around them.

"Both."

His answer left my curiosity piqued. "I bet you came with a girl. You're the kind of guy who looks like you'd never be alone."

"Are you sure about that? I'm taking construction engineering. I'm about this close to showing my math professor what I look like when I'm pissed off."

I laughed. "Sounds like me with my English professor. Can I be honest?"

"Sure—although I don't know why you'd try to slip a lie past me."

Yeah the truth was in my scent, in my breaths. I was exposed to him. "In the fall I thought a new start outside of a small town would be good, but college has been overwhelming at times."

He nodded. I couldn't see his face.

I kept going. "It's not even the coursework. It's the humans...I guess I've lived in a small town for too long."

"Humans are the same anywhere you go. Adapting is hard, but I believe you're more than capable."

Talking seemed the best way to fill the time so I kept the conversation going. It was nice to learn more about him. "When was the last time you came here with family?" I asked him.

"A long time ago but I came here with my old man."

Now that was someone I knew personally. Every werewolf in South Toms River knew him. As the pack leader, his father controlled the pack with an iron paw. He didn't tolerate having weak members slow us down, and I considered myself one of those people.

Just thinking about that man soured my mood, but when I took in my surroundings again those bitter feelings faded. The forest floor began to clear up and now rocky outcroppings peppered the landscape. Hills, and even mountains covered in greenery, stretched out in the distance. This kind of place reminded me a bit of Double Trouble State Park.

We walked for what seemed like an hour or so before I smelled burnt wood, but there wasn't any sign of a smoke trail in the air. No one was there.

We traveled uphill for a bit until we reached a clearing.

"Wow." I glanced around.

"Isn't it perfect?" he asked.

I nodded. We could see for miles in every direction. Even the Fourth Run creek he'd mentioned earlier. We'd walked a long way, and we couldn't see the campgrounds or the parking lot anymore. We were truly alone.

It was about time.

"So you and your dad used to setup camp here?" I asked him.

He nodded. "A very long time ago."

I checked out the camp. A set of rocks formed a large circle around a firepit. There were already ideal spots for tent placement. Smaller trees nearby could provide kindling.

"How come more people haven't used this spot? I smell only werewolves here."

"Humans have used this spot before, but not too often. During the winter, the wind gets really cold and brisk. During the summer time, they aren't many places for shade so anybody who comes here will get baked."

"Crispy humans..."

He chuckled. "I guess you could say that."

With only my backpack to keep me company, I tried to play things cool as Thorn began assembling our tenet. Yep, you heard that right. There was only one tent for the both of us.

"How many people can sleep in there?" I asked as I began to gather tinder for a fire. Standing there watching him work would only make me more nervous.

"There's enough room for two to three." The small smile he gave me set my heart aflutter.

"You're not a cover hog, are you?" I had to say something to keep things light.

"I like to stay warm. You gonna help me do that?"

I shook my head with a grin.

Thorn finished the tent while I placed large pieces of wood in the firepit. I wished I had more things. Like a tea pot, a sweater, more clothes, a pot in case I wanted to check something...

"Hey Nat, could you come here for a second?"

I found Thorn getting the fire going. "What's up?"

"How long you gonna sit over there by yourself?"

"Just doing an inventory check."

"As long as you're not studying."

I snorted. "I have the notorious Dr. Foster this semester. If I'm smart, before the semester is over I'll figure out a way to study in my sleep."

"Professor Freak Out?"

"That's him."

Thorn laughed. "I know someone who had him in the fall. The guy said he's traumatized from all the homework he had."

"All the other sociology classes were full so I'm stuck with Professor Foster."

"My condolences."

I shrugged. "I do fine."

"I got that idea. You always seem to keep to yourself at the library or a nook somewhere."

I was crouched, and he used his index finger to push against my shoulder.

"Hey!" I fell over with a laugh.

Our fun ended when a few hot pieces of wood sparked and leapt out of the pit. Thorn jumped over and stomped them out.

I had questions, but I'd held them in. We had a whole two days out here and the thought of being here without knowing why he asked me to come with him was unnerving. He could've gone home. He could've stayed on campus and figured out how he'd hunt outside of the city. And yet, for some reason, he didn't do that. He wanted me here with him.

"So...Thorn," I managed to ask. "I was wondering how come—"

The sound of others' voices cut me off. It wasn't just one voice either. I caught three women and one man. The moment they came over the hill and approached our camp, my assessment was correct.

Two blondes, in nothing more than T-shirts and cut-off shorts, approached the camp first. One was leggier and taller, with a dominant air about her. The two people behind them were a man and a brunette.

All four of them were werewolves.

Shit.

"Hey Thorn, you beat us here," the guy yelled.

Thorn nodded their way. His back was to me—for which I was grateful. I wouldn't want him to see the agitation tightening my face. Why didn't he tell me others were coming? The werewolves had backpacks and gear. Which meant they planned to camp out with us.

The dark-haired werewolf walked up to Thorn and shook his hand. "Long time no see."

"I honestly didn't think you'd come," Thorn replied. "You keep canceling on me. It's been what? Five years since the pack leader gathering, Perry?"

"Pretty much. Having the pack leaders meet more often than that is asking for a nuclear war." Perry was as tall as Thorn, but not as handsome. He has the same long legs, lean arms, and grace the son of pack leaders have, but in the way that Thorn was calm and self-assured, Perry gave off a happy-go-lucky vibe I envied.

"So when you gonna say hi to me?" the prettier blonde in a pink shirt and shorts asked Thorn.

"What's up, Erica." Thorn nodded her way.

I held back my smile. He didn't just open up to anyone.

"Who's the stranger?" Perry looked in my direction.

"Oh, everyone, this is Natalya. She's from my hometown and goes to Pitt." He turned to point to the others. "Nat, this is Perry Vaughn and his girlfriend Erica Holden. Behind them is Becky Knoll and Cassie Zimmerman."

Once he'd said her name, I knew who the blonde was.

"You're from South Toms River?" she asked me.

I nodded.

"Something about you seemed familiar," she said, "but I couldn't place it."

Which meant I was as memorable as a used dishrag.

Werewolf packs are hierarchical. Those with strong positions in the upper tiers, like Thorn or Erica, rarely associated with someone like me who was about as high as a rogue.

Perry and Thorn began to chat while Becky and Cassie sat down near the fire. Instead of joining her friends, Erica stood in front of me, effectively blocking my view. She slid her arm around her boyfriend's waist, but her gaze settled appreciatively on Thorn.

Her hip was tilted to the side, revealing an enticing curve. From her full breasts to her bottom that almost peeked out from under her designer jean shorts, Erica projected perfection.

When she turned around she glanced at me. Her bright

smile faded and was replaced with something else: indif-ference.

For the first time in a long time, I had felt beautiful and had hope for something more in my life.

With a single gorgeous smile, Erica Holden snatched that feeling away from me.

CHAPTER 3

THE LOOK on Erica's face could've been a harbinger of the beginning of the end. For me, I saw it as a challenge. I still wanted him.

A dominant female, who already had a man, had given me a subtle signal. It might seem strange, but werewolf females use signals to communicate. Even human women are the same. We have expressions we give each other like a herd of female elephants. We do things to keep each other in line. A man might think an open smile from one woman to another was a gesture of kindness, but if he looked deeper, he'd discover it could be something else entirely. It was all about body language and women read each other as well as men.

When Erica glanced at me, then turned her head, as well as her whole body to block my view, she projected a crystal clear message: *stay back, stay hidden, I can have whomever I please.*

So I sat next to my backpack and waited for the right opportunity to slip out of my lower rank.

The afternoon turned to evening. Perry pulled out a

portable grill and Thorn prepared burgers. They laughed and chatted among themselves. This scene to me seemed surreal. Hadn't I seen past pack events where the dominant wolves sat together and those in the lower ranks waited around them for scraps? No matter the age of the werewolf, we naturally fell in line.

Until Thorn called for me.

"You want a beer, Nat?" Instead of waiting for me to say no, he tossed me one.

I looked at the can as if he'd tossed me an atomic bomb. I wasn't too fond of beer. I was more of a wine person, but I would drink it if that was all I had.

"Nat, you shouldn't drink that cheap shit," Becky said to me.

"Let her drink it," Erica said. "It's probably what she's *used* to."

"This isn't some country club outing," Perry said to Becky.

Thorn crossed the clearing to the other side, grabbed my arm, and then pulled me toward the fire. I was about to place a towel on the ground, but he beat me to it. "There you go. It's much easier to chat with you if you're near the fire, you know."

"I know." Already I'd taken the role I was supposed to have. I wasn't looking him in the face anymore. After being with the humans for months and away from my family, the pack life had almost been forgotten. Just a few hours and I was back in the same place that reminded me how low I was.

He sat down next to me at the fire. His side warmed mine.

Becky and Perry weren't done with their conversation.

"I have to watch what I'm doing all the time," Becky

said. "I wish I could stay at Mount Holyoke forever. At least when I'm there I don't have to think about some asshole my parents will setup as my husband."

"You won't end up with someone as distinguished as Perry," Erica said bluntly, "but I'm sure you won't want for anything."

Becky gave her friend the finger. I wish I could do it, too. What did Perry see in her anyway?

Erica played with a strand of her glossy hair. "The Holdens are moving up the ranks and my dad says once I marry I can move to D.C. permanently."

"If we get married," Perry added.

"Oh, stop. You know you like me." She sauntered up to him, running her manicured hands down his chest. I had to glance away before I vomited.

Perry chuckled and pulled her close. He ran his hands down her back until he cupped her bottom.

"Okay, keep the R-rated stuff for the tent," Thorn said with a smile.

The two exchanged kisses before Erica found a place to sit at the fire—right next to Thorn. Perry sat on her other side. Wow, this chick was no joke. Her scent and body didn't betray her intentions, but to me, what she wanted was loud and clear.

Thorn, on the other hand, looked out into the darkness. His attention seemed elsewhere.

"Is everything alright?" I asked him. There seemed to be nothing out there. Just the sounds of nocturnal wildlife emerging from their burrows. The wind was clear. On the way I hadn't seen any suspicious tracks. My dad, one of the best trackers in the northeast, had taught me well.

I touched his shoulder and he stiffened.

"Sorry," I blurted.

"It's probably the full moon." He bumped his shoulder with mine. "My skin itches tonight."

"I know the feeling," I admitted. Right now I felt the pull of the moon too, but the wary vibes I got off him were bothersome.

"So Thorn, what plans do you have after Pitt?" Erica asked him with a grin.

He shrugged. "I dunno yet. I guess whatever my old man wants me to do."

"He won't be in command forever. Sooner or later, you'll be the king…" She leaned toward him and Thorn gave me the side-eye as if to say, *"Can you save me?"*

The sad grin I gave back conveyed, *"I'm a life raft that will sink you, buddy."*

Soon enough, the burgers were done and everyone ate. After that Becky made s'mores and she handed them out. Well, everyone got one after Thorn passed me his. Becky had skipped giving me one altogether.

As Thorn was making another one, he abruptly put the stick down and came to me. He leaned close to my ear, eliciting a shiver out of me. His whisper was so low, I had to strain everything else out to hear him.

"Pack your bag, Nat." I moved back from having him so close, but he grabbed my shoulder.

"Wha?"

"Just do it." He touched my cheek. "Don't worry. I got you. Right?"

I nodded.

"That's my girl."

I wiped off my hands and picked up the towel I left on the ground.

"Where's she going?" Cassie asked Erica.

"I don't care," she replied. "Maybe to bed."

I ignored the comments and kept going. I glanced into the darkness, seeing nothing. Why was Thorn so upset? I ran to my pack and began gathering the items I'd pulled out. My sleeping bag. The sanitary wipes I placed beside them. The sweater I planned to wear when I lay next to Thorn.

A yip drew my attention toward the bonfire. The others scattered.

Something had entered the clearing.

CHAPTER 4

Rogue werewolves tore through the clearing. Dozens of males emerged from the shadows. Thorn and I had made a grave error. The rogues had grown in numbers and now we were in the wrong place at the wrong time. With two dominant males in our group to boot.

Werewolves roaming without a pack leader to guide them lived on mostly instinct. Many lived outside of the cities and kept to themselves—unless they gathered in enough numbers to form another pack.

"Kill the men," I heard a man yell. "Subdue the females!"

One burst through our tent and grabbed me by the arm. I snarled and snapped at him, but he didn't let me go. He tried to drag me toward the edge of the clearing, but I dug in my heels and yanked back hard.

"Pretty female," the dark-haired man sneered.

Fyodor Stravinsky hadn't raised a wilting flower.

Also, this rotten bastard smelled god-awful, and he'd grabbed me with a slimy hand. Instead of dwelling on the wet stuff that slid down my arm, I sprang on him. We crashed to the grass and tumbled a bit, getting tangled in arms and legs while he tried to subdue me and I tried to punch his face.

His arms got close to my mouth. The scrappy wolf in me lurched in to bite, but I cringed instead. Thankfully, my wolf won and I bit his ass.

"Bitch!" The rogue grabbed me by the neck and shook hard. All around us, more fighting erupted. Where was Thorn? Was he all right?

I tried to look to the right toward the clearing, but the grip on my neck was tightening.

With effort I managed to free my legs and I kicked him hard in his junk. The rogue grimaced and released my neck. That brief pause was long enough for me to swing my elbow across his chin. Once his head came down, I slammed my clasped fists onto the middle of his back. That sweet spot always took my younger brother down. Once my attacker fell over, I thought I was free, but another rogue came for me. I sprinted off into the darkness. Like the fool I was, I'd forgotten we were uphill. Naturally, I stumbled down the hill, hitting almost everything on the way down.

A rock on the side of my neck. (Hello, hard place.)

The unforgiving ground scraped skin on my back. (Carpet burn, anyone?)

And finally the *coup de grâce*, I crashed into a tree in the pitch-black forest below the clearing.

Oh, God I was messed up. Stars swam along my peripheral vision, but I forced myself to get up and keep going.

"Don't lay low, Natalya," my dad would say. *"Enemies are on nipping at your tail."*

I'd always had a strong bark, but a weak bite. At this moment, I questioned whether I'd be biting anything again.

Once I got to my feet, nausea hit and a cold sweat blanketed my back. I wobbled a bit and stumbled forward on unsteady feet. Not far from me, the fighting continued.

Go back, Nat, I said to myself. *Check on Thorn.* The wolf in me had tasted blood and was eager to jump back in. I thought about returning, but Thorn would be pissed.

He'd told me to grab my pack—which I no longer had —and run.

I stood there for a moment, unsure what to do. I decided it was best to make a run for it. I pulled out my hair tie and left it on the ground for Thorn to track. Then I escaped.

After running for a while, all the beer and s'mores caught up with me. My hard sprint turned into a tired ass jog. The moon was gone. Cloud cover made it hard for me to see. The shadows blended in together. I couldn't see what I stepped in or what I touched.

With step I made, my panic rose higher.

A little voice, the one I kept locked away in the back of my mind, whispered that it had to have its way. I was filthy and I'd never be clean again. That filth was the reason other pack members didn't respect me. It was the reason why I was flawed. The only way to be free was to scrub away any foreign matter until my skin bled if necessary. The wolf never won over this voice no matter now hard I tried.

Thorn, I'm so sorry, I thought. Why couldn't I be stronger for you and stand with you?

Things got even more fun. Rain began to fall. Now I was wet, cold, and leaning on a tree in the middle of a panic attack. I pressed my back against the hard wood.

As I began to wheeze, I pressed harder, hoping to distract myself as my lungs constricted.

Werewolves shouldn't be like this.

Werewolves shouldn't be like this.

And yet I was.

I pushed my back against the tree hard enough for the knobs in the wood to stab me, but it didn't help.

The arms that reached out for me and enveloped me did though.

"Gotcha, babe," Thorn whispered.

I was at just the right height for him to lay his chin on top of my head. My arms were pressed against his chest, and his thundering heartbeat vibrated along my cold fingers. Peace settled through me.

"Thorn..." The sound seemed far away even though I'd said it.

"I'm here." He pulled me back a bit to feel for injuries. "I smell blood. You okay?" In empty darkness, I could only smell him and feel him checking my arms and legs.

"It's not mine."

"Okay, good." He was shaking. Not from the cold, but from anger. The bitter smell was seeping out of him.

"Is everyone else..."

"I think they got away. There were too many of them to tell." He urged me to head in the direction I was going in. Farther away from camp. "When that guy said there were a few rogues, I had no idea he meant they had enough to form a pack. There were too many to defend against." He cursed and used a word my uncle Boris rarely said.

"I'm so sorry, Nat," he added.

"What do you have to be sorry about?"

"I should have made us leave sooner." He sighed. "I knew something was wrong. I could feel it, but I wasn't listening to my instincts."

The way he stiffened when I touched him made me flinch.

"Don't apologize. I'm fine." I really wasn't to be honest. At all.

"You don't look like it."

I snorted as he pulled me to keep going north. I loved how he held my hand. "How can you see anything out here?"

"Right now I can't see much, but I can 'feel' what's ahead if that helps."

"Oh really? Are you hiding the fact you're a spellcaster or something?" I joked.

He laughed. A sound I needed to hear. "Are you asking if I have some magic tricks up my sleeve?"

"Maybe." The temptation to glance around was strong. Werewolves didn't discuss magic. Even in the middle of nowhere. If Grandma mentioned magic, Mom always looked at her like she said a bad word. She hated magic and those associated with it—the warlocks, witches, and wizards. She told me werewolves couldn't cast spells and the Code was put in place to protect us.

Grandma had other words on the matter.

"The Code? Pfft!" Grandma Lasovskaya would laugh. *"A bunch of rules for people who are still afraid of their own shadow."*

"Have you ever seen a werewolf cast a spell before?" I asked Thorn.

"Seen what?" He was walking faster now.

"Werewolves *using* magic?" So far talking was good for me. It helped me not think about the growing pain along my neck where I'd hit that rock. The burns along my back weren't as bad, but I'd gotten myself good when I'd slammed into that rock.

More time passed. Thorn had been quiet for too long.

"You have seen it before!" I hissed. "I thought that was nothing more than a legend."

"It is a legend. You should obey the Code, Nat. It's there to protect us for a reason."

He was lying to me and had tried to play with words. When werewolves didn't want to outright lie, they gave statements that were true, gave a question in response, or just didn't answer period.

Thorn Grantham had lied to me. *Interesting.*

"We need to find a place to lay low for a while," he said.

"Lay low with what? We don't have any backpacks or a even tent."

His grip on my hand loosened, and he played with my fingers until they open so he could intertwine them. "We're werewolves. I think we can last out here in the wilderness."

"What about bears?" I asked.

"Haven't smelled any."

"Wolves?"

"*Seriously?*"

"What if we get lost?" I gestured around us.

"Would Fyodor Stravinsky's daughter get lost in the woods?"

I rolled my eyes. "In the dark without the stars and the moon she would."

This was rather embarrassing. I had the opportunity to make the Stravinskys proud and I was looking for every reason to fail.

Thorn pulled me to move faster. "I see something ahead that should be a good place for us to hunker down for the night. We've added about two miles between us and the camp."

We'd made it that far, huh? Everything I valued was so far away. I could almost remember the weight of the pack on my back. The secure feeling of knowing my belongings were close by.

"Maybe we should go back and check for the others?" I asked.

"Nat, you came here because of me, and I need to protect you. Perry and Erica are stronger than you think. Also, he's alpha material. If we made it out of there, they all did."

Was it bad of me to hope the rogues pushed Erica down a peg or two in terms of her attitude? I doubted it.

What Thorn saw was nothing more than a thicket of bushes and a few trees that formed a tight circle. The clouds had parted a bit, leaving me a view I wish I couldn't see. So far I'd managed to ignore the squishy sounds my tennis shoes made as I walked through the grass, but now that the moonlight spilled through the cracks in the clouds, I could see the pools along the ground and drops falling from the trees. When I glanced back to look in the direction we'd come from, I noticed our footprints had avoided the puddles.

He could see somehow...and he'd avoided the puddles for me.

I tried to swallow down the strange honeyed feeling stirring in my stomach.

"This isn't the best accommodations, but at least everything is quiet." He sat, discarded his shirt, and placed it on the ground next to him. "Rest a bit."

I eased down and forced myself not to cringe. I had enough bruises to last for a while.

His shirt was slightly damp, but I didn't complain. Seeing Thorn Grantham without his shirt was worth it. I tried not to stare, but the way his shoulder muscles flexed and his pecs twitched were enough eye candy to keep my sweet tooth happy for days to come. My eyes wandered over his stomach, almost wishing my hands could've done the wandering. His abs seemed to have no end. Thorn was a beautiful specimen.

I briefly closed my eyes, unable to stop thinking about him. I could still feel him holding me, my nose pressed against his collarbone. He had no idea how he tortured me just sitting there quietly.

I had to say something. "So we wait until dawn?"

"Yeah, then I get us out of here safely."

For a moment, even with all the drama, I realized this short vacation was about to be over before it had even started. We couldn't stay out here without any supplies or food—yet I wanted more time with him like this. Yes, I seriously said that.

"Are you hungry?" he asked. "I could find us some food."

I shook my head. Even if I was starving, I didn't want him to leave my side. "I'm just tired."

"This isn't much of a blanket, but you're welcome to lay on it."

I tried to curl up on his shirt, but there wasn't much real estate.

"Just a sec." He lay down next to me, then gestured for me to lay closer.

"What do you want me...?" I asked.

He patted his shoulder. "Put your head here. We can share body heat and you can lay comfortably on my shirt."

I lay next to him, conscious of every hard muscle he had. His side muscles were unyielding, and when I pressed the side of my face against his pec, I melted into warm goo.

"That's nice..." The words snuck out of my mouth.

"You like what you see, huh?"

"I mean it's *nice* place to rest. Who wants to sleep on a hard shoulder?"

"So you're saying you don't like the way I look?" His grin was infectious.

My mouth opened and closed like a landlocked fish. "You're perfect—what I mean is I think you look *nice*."

He stopped smiling and I swallowed hard when he said, "Well, I think you look more than nice."

My heartbeat quickened to the point of painful. What made my cheeks even warmer was the fact he could hear my body's reaction. He'd know by my quickened breath how much his words stirred my passions.

"You're sweet, Thorn, but I know how I look compared to some of the girls on campus."

He tilted his head as if in thought. "True, you are different. Your clothes aren't as tight."

"Is that what you like?" I could tell he'd turned his head my way, but I couldn't look at him.

"How come I don't often see you wearing those tight skirts?"

I finally looked at him, ready to punch his exposed stomach. "Skirts aren't comfortable during the winter."

His lips had parted slightly. The moonlight had turned his blue eyes purple and his blond hair gray. Even cast in shadows he was perfect. Practically ethereal.

"I like skirts," he whispered. "Especially when you wear them. You drive me crazy every time you do."

He'd seen me wearing them before? When? Every day I thought I blended into the crowd, and yet someone had been looking at me from afar.

"Natalya." My name was a heated whisper as he brought his head toward me. Next came his lips, a brief brush against mine. I trembled. He was still there, a hairsbreadth away. I'd been kissed before, but not like this. Finally, I couldn't take it anymore and our mouths collided.

I'd never had this delicious rush surging from my stomach to between my legs. I'd never felt like I was about to float away from one kiss.

Thorn's hand reached down to cup my face. He explored my mouth, nibble by nibble. My hands continued to rest against his side, but as our kissed deepened, I grew bold and placed them on his chest. His skin was scalding, and his quickened heartbeat thrummed against my fingers.

He wanted me as much as I wanted him.

When he finally withdrew though, I felt a sense of loss, but he smiled and shifted me to lay my head back on his shoulder.

"If we keep going like this, I will be distracted until dawn." His voice was hoarse with need. "I should guard us. Get some sleep if you can."

After what happened, I doubted I'd sleep one wink.

WE SLEPT IN FOR A WHILE. When I woke up, the noonday sun greeted me. Waking up next to Thorn was a fantasy I'd had countless times since we'd met in the class registration line. And who wouldn't? Especially with a man as hot as he was.

I fell asleep not long after we'd kissed, but now that I was awake and he slept softly beside me, a new fantasy circled my head: Could this be real between us and not a spring break fling?

I wasn't a fool. At Pitt folks hooked up all the time. Why wouldn't werewolves be any different?

Hope is such a fragile thing and I want to cling to it. Like any girl, I imagined what it would be like if we went back to South Toms River as boyfriend and girlfriend. As the next in line to become pack leader, Thorn would be respected. I'd get the same treatment. We'd live together in town and I'd take him to my noisy family gatherings. I smiled at the pleasant thought.

That pleasant feeling faded though as Thorn got up.

"We need to start moving again," he said with a yawn.

"Now that it's daylight, we don't know if they're tracking us or not. We should run into the Pennsylvania Turnpike sooner or later."

"What reason do they have to follow us?"

"If the rogues are gathering numbers, they wouldn't want other wolves like us pissing in their backyard. Especially if their alpha has a tenuous hold on the pack and the younger males are looking for females."

So we continued north. I waited for Thorn to take my hand, but he didn't. As the day passed, I didn't see anything other than more than more hills and mountains.

"This place is beautiful," I said to break up the silence. I wanted him to kiss me again, but I was too shy to bring up the subject. "All these trees remind me of the woods around your family's cabin."

Ahead of me, he nodded. "Yeah, it kind of does. Most of the time, I try to forget about that house—I think of my mom when I do."

"I'm sorry, I didn't mean to stir up bad memories." I didn't know much about his mom. Only that she died after his brother Will was born. I'd heard from others she was very beautiful and kind-hearted.

He slowed down and kept pace with me. "It's all right. I like to think about her sometimes."

"Did you ever run with her during the full moon?"

He nodded. "Once we'd run here. Those were better times before my old man took over the pack." He picked up a rock and threw it stiffly over the trees. "When he became alpha everything was about appearances. How others would perceive him through his offspring. Even his *pregnant* wife. He expected her to step up to the plate when others challenged her for the position. She was forced to fight not long after my brother had been born."

Thorn's voice grew quiet. "I hate thinking about him."

I sucked in a breath and an uncomfortable feeling settled into my stomach. I wanted to know more about what happened to her, but Thorn had to be feeling worse.

"I still wish I could've met her," I said.

He finally smiled. "You remind me of her. You have a quiet inner strength like she did."

After that we walked in silence until twilight painted the cloudy sky. Our pace was slow. Neither of us cared about where we went, only that we got a moment of peace.

"Just a few more hours until the full moon," Thorn remarked.

"Before the attack I'd been looking forward to tonight. I've never shared the full moon with anyone before." Just my family.

"Have you ever had a boyfriend?"

I cringed and scrambled to think of a witty answer. I've never had sex, and I could count the number of dates I'd had on one hand. Of course his question could be completely innocent, but he had to be like most of the guys at Pitt. Half horny, half hungry all the time.

"I've dated..." Without having a single steady boyfriend. Being a loner didn't make me the best girlfriend material.

"Dated? Meaning...A few months? A year or two?" He grinned devilishly. "I guess you're too much for most guys, huh?"

"Yep, too much... " Too much wasn't the right word. I was inadequate. Maybe on the outside Thorn thought Natalya Stravinsky was a force to be reckoned with, but on the inside I was far too fragile.

Shame spilled over me as we decided to begin our full moon hunt on a hill overlooking a small lake. I hadn't told him about my mental illness and I never planned to do it.

This illusion I'd created was something I didn't want to shatter. I didn't mind letting him think I had quirks. Didn't all of us have peculiar habits we kept?

On my worse days when I didn't want to look in the mirror, I felt like Thorn Grantham deserved better. Now the sun was setting and soon we'd face each other in our true form. Would he sense my true nature as well?

Grandma Lasovskaya had told me when I was younger that I'd find my mate for life in wolf form. She'd fallen for my *dedushka* during a full moon. Encountering a white wolf was rare, and somehow on a chilly spring day she met one.

I touched my chin to my chest. Would he find my body beautiful? A tinge began along my spine. The change was coming.

"You gonna take your clothes off?" Thorn asked casually. He took a spot in front of me, forcing me to look at him.

Heat filled my face. This should be the easy part. I've undressed in front of countless people. Becoming a wolf was our nature. And yet, I couldn't look him in the eyes as I shrugged off my shirt.

"There," I said proudly and crossed my arms.

"I'm curious to see how you're gonna run in those pants."

I rolled my eyes. My hands rested on my waistband. Thorn reached over and rubbed the back of his hand against my bare stomach. I quivered in response.

Deftly, he unbuttoned my jeans. "There you go..." His voice was lower now, coarser. The sliver of control he had was fading as well as mine. My bones flexed and pulsed. My breath grew heavy in my lungs. I couldn't sense the wolf within me anymore. We were one.

Finally, my pants came off. He did the same. All that

remained were my panties and bra. I slipped those off and stood before him as naked as the day I was born.

He was the same. And how *magnificent* he was. My gaze lingered on lean muscular legs, up to a hard stomach and finally to his face. The dark look in his eyes dared me not to look away.

He was *turned* on. It was impossible to miss down there. Really.

My hands moved of their own volition and I covered my nakedness.

"Don't." He pulled my hands away. "I want to see all of you."

He lessened the distance between us. A part of me wanted him to touch me. To reach for me and quench the hunger I had for him since I'd met him.

"I c-can't believe I'm acting shy like this," I stammered. "It's not as if others haven't seen my *sad* naked body."

His laugh was deep and unsettled me. "It's not sad at all. I'm sure you can tell parts of me are *standing* with applause."

That made me spit out a laugh.

His hand hovered near the sensitive skin under my skin, but he formed a fist instead and withdrew. "You're blushing all over. You act like you've never been naked in front of a man before."

Should I try to go around the truth? I gave in. "Hunting is one thing. This is completely different. I've always had clothes on when...making out."

"You've had sex fully clothed?"

At that point I wished the moon's effects would kick in any time now. "Thorn, I've never had sex before. I've had *lots* of opportunities but—" And now I sounded like I was a freak of the week. *Stop talking now, Nat, before you make things worse.*

"Whether you've had sex or not doesn't matter," he whispered. "I'll be honest though. The fact I could mark you as mine and only mine makes me want you even more."

I bit my lip. That was the hottest thing I'd ever heard in my life. He'd left me speechless. I closed my eyes and clenched my fists. The desire was there, but there was no time to act. Only time to feel the delicious tension coursing through me.

"I'm not done with you yet, Natalya," he breathed. "We'll deal with concluding this *conversation* later."

The time had come. I could feel it. My bones were beginning to collapse, bend, and contort until I became my true form. The whole process was painful each and every time, but tonight was different. Anticipation dulled each break. Budding pleasure made the searing heat in my limbs endurable.

As we ran off together into the night, I told myself this run would be perfect. I wouldn't be sitting alone in apartment. I was with someone and we'd explore this forest together.

CHAPTER 6

THE MORNING after running with a pack is like coming down from a massive high. I'd never been so content.

I looked around. The shadow of trees obscured our view of the sky, but the rising sun was coming. I didn't want to get up. Thorn's hand rested on my hip. His front pressed against my back. My whole body hummed, just thinking of feeling his hands all over me.

He growled as his hand clenched my hip, and his hips pulsed against my backside. Nervous flutters danced across my stomach. I sighed and closed my eyes tightly.

Why was I so nervous right now? Wasn't this what I wanted? To be alone with Thorn and have his body so close to mine we could almost be one.

Being a virgin sucked.

"Turn around, Nat," he whispered against the back of my neck.

"What happens if I do?"

"A kiss."

"That's it?"

"Would you like for it to be?"

The way he gripped my hips told me that wasn't the case.

I wanted him to take my virginity and run away with it. I wanted him to make this yearning go away—but a kiss was one thing and sex was another. Werewolves mated and humans *fucked*. I wasn't fond of that word, but it conveyed the truth.

"You've gone quiet on me," he said.

"Thinking."

"About what?" He kissed my neck.

"Aren't we just here to run? I didn't expect to do this so soon...Hmmmm... " His hand had crept up to my breast and my body melted like a willing traitor. "...after we kissed."

"When we do anything in our relationship doesn't matter," he said simply. "It's *why* we do it."

Good point. "And why would we ruin our friendship with a one night stand?" I frowned. "One morning stand?"

He kissed my shoulder and pulled my hair to the side to expose more of my neck. "What makes you think I just want to be your friend?"

"I can't answer that." Any other questions would prove difficult with all the places he was touching. He turned me around.

"How do I prove this isn't a one time thing? That I've been thinking about you and me ever since we met in that registration line a few months ago."

I didn't know what to say.

He lightly kissed my lips. "Maybe I should tell you about all the times I've thought about you. The times when you didn't think I could see you walking across campus. You might think no one truly saw you, but I did. When I lived in South Toms River I wished we could have gotten to know each other. I feel like I missed out on falling for you sooner."

My stomach flipped, only to flip again. Thorn Grantham kept leaving me speechless.

He continued. "I believe fate brought us together in that line. When I think about how I lost my car keys and ended up getting in line later—at that very moment you were in front of me—it seems like we were fated to meet. To come together." He shuddered and stretched out on top of me.

Our lips met again. This time his touch was commanding and unyielding. Doubt swam away as he kissed my lips. My neck. My collarbone to my breasts. His featherlight caresses rained down my belly to down to the place I never expected a man to kiss me.

Our bodies finally became one, and he refused to let me look away. He nipped at my lips when I closed my eyes.

"Look at me, babe, " he said softly. "I want to see how beautiful you are."

His heat matched my heat. It was everything I'd wished for.

As we both peaked he whispered words so tenderly I barely caught them: "You belong to me now, Natalya Stravinsky."

Maybe I was imagining things, but I never knew this act would make me feel so complete. So loved.

Until the very end I hadn't looked away. I fell in love headfirst and didn't look back.

CHAPTER 7

A few hours later, Thorn and I walked hand and hand back to the spot by the lake where we'd left our clothes.

Unfortunately, they were now *gone*.

"No way," I groaned.

Thorn settled for a curse and then took off to do a sweep. He came back empty-handed. Wow, that dampened the mood. First rogues had attacked our camp, we made a run for it without supplies, and now someone had taken our clothes.

At least we had nothing left to take. Positive thinking, right?

"Who would've stolen them?" I asked with a dry laugh.

He shrugged. "I don't know. I guess there's a woodland creature strutting around the forest with two pairs of jeans and some shirts."

I looked down at my nakedness. Was I gonna have to weave myself some clothes? "The original plan won't work if we're like this. Two folks walking down a highway butt naked is illegal."

"No, we won't. We'll double back and try out the campground with the humans. If that doesn't pan out…"

I made a motion for him to continue. "And if that doesn't pan out we'll…"

"We'll be sneaking back to the car," he finished.

I sighed and started walking without him. He'd catch up. It wasn't his fault we'd lost our clothes, but I was still irked.

Hours later, it took us forever to reach the campgrounds. The sun was low in the sky by the time I saw smoke trails—a sure sign humans camped nearby.

"I wish we could go back to the clearing and get our backpacks," I said.

"I do, too. A lot of that stuff I borrowed from someone else."

"When can we get them back?"

"Do you want to walk up there without a stitch of clothing on and see how well negotiations go with the rogues?"

"Would it hurt to try?"

He blew out a long breath. "Before you get any ideas I'm not letting them see you naked. Right now you smell good enough to eat. You're mine now. No dice."

That made me grin. "So what do we do now?"

We ended up stealing from the humans.

Sneaking into to the campground without being seen was quite the adventure. Even with twilight on our side. We ran from tree to tree, trying to make sure our naked bits didn't get flashed to folks.

"How about that car?" He pointed to the first target: a truck with an RV attached.

"They smell young."

We took positions to search the back of the truck, but

our luck ran out when young couple left the RV to start grilling. And the lady was the perfect size and height too. The guy not so much. We dodged a bullet with that one. Thorn wouldn't be able to get one leg into the man's short jeans.

Finding another source wasn't easy. We went from one camper to another and couldn't find much. It wasn't like the old days where folks left their unmentionables out. Finally, we were forced to get Thorn a pair of oversized jeans and a T-shirt that had been left on a line outside a camper, while I grabbed a sundress someone had discarded after swimming. All of the clothes didn't smell good, but our options at this point were limited.

Night had fallen again by the time we headed for Thorn's black SUV. I stopped short on the way when I realized something. "Ugh, we are so stupid! How are you gonna drive us anywhere, Grantham?"

His slow grin filled his beautiful face. "I've been caught naked more often than you can imagine." He chuckled. "Once burned, once learned." When we were outside his car, he scooted underneath, and after a bit, he emerged with a small magnetic box holding backup keys.

Just seeing the keys inside filled me with relief. Already I could feel a hot shower pouring down my back.

Camping is so overrated.

I WAS BACK in my dorm room. Just being back was bittersweet. I had my personal things around me—at least my suitcase since I'd left it in the SUV. But as I sat in my room, having just stepped through the door, I wished I would've said something more to him other than, "Talk to you later."

I could've been suave and said, "Hey, come up for a while."

Or maybe, "What are you doing tonight?"

What sounded even better was, "Let's have wild hot monkey sex in my dorm room."

None of those cool statements came out of my mouth. Instead of even trying to kiss him, I got nervous, I said my goodbyes, and I ran away.

I rested my hands in my face. "Why am I like this?"

I tossed my suitcase on my bed and noticed the light on my answering machine was blinking. A rarity.

I hit play.

Thorn laughed came through the speaker. "I can't believe you just left me like that, Nat." He sighed through the phone, and I got closer to the machine. "I waited for five minutes to see if you'd come back out, but you didn't. Now, I'm not a man to chase after women. Maybe you'll call me, maybe you won't, but at least I hope you'll open your door."

Open the door?

I turned to look at the dark wooden door on the other side of the room. Was he really behind it?

I quickly crossed the space and checked. There he was waiting for me.

He leaned against the doorframe with his arms crossed.

"Hey, you," he said softly.

"Hey..."

He captured my lips before I had a chance to speak. By the time we parted I was breathless.

"You left so fast," he said "I know this trip didn't go well, but it wasn't that bad, was it?"

"Not really." I shrugged. "I guess I ran out of words to say. I'm scared to be honest."

A few girls passed behind him in the hallway, but he didn't move. "Why?"

"I'm not that good at this relationship thing. Also I'm not your type, Thorn. I'm flawed." I swallowed the lump growing inside my throat. "I have obsessive compulsive disorder and it affects my life a lot." There I said it. After the words came out a weight lifted off my shoulders—but my heart grew heavy instead. My shame was now out in the open.

"I knew that already, babe," he said softly.

I couldn't speak for a bit. "*Really?*"

He pulled me close, and the sigh I let out turned into a content hum. Then I recalled all the things he'd done for me: the towels on the ground, avoiding the puddles, and the way he protected me whenever he could. "Remember when

I told you I'd been watching you for a while? I've seen it, but I don't care."

He caressed the side of my face. "You're beautifully flawed and you're just what I need. What I've always needed in my life."

We had a bit of a crowd now, but Thorn hadn't let me go.

"So what do we do now?" I asked him.

Finally, he closed the door behind him. "You got any plans today?"

I smiled brightly. "With you I do."

The End

GRANDMA'S DATE NIGHT

CHAPTER 1

Reader Note: This story takes place after Compelled
(Coveted #3)

SOUTH TOMS RIVER, New Jersey, swarmed with busybodies. If you checked under the nearest rock, you'd find one lounging there in wait, hungry for any juicy information a *complete* stranger would need to know.

Werewolf busybodies were mostly the same—they just happened to spread your business to other werewolves at the pack hunts during the full moon. What differed between the two was how you warded them off.

It just so happened while I was taking Grandma Lasovskaya out for lunch, a rampant gossip spotted us. Even at the diner in the next town off the Garden State Parkway, I should've known I wouldn't find peace. Not that I disliked Renissa Delaney-Danford—yes, everyone from South Toms River used her whole name—but at the ripe old age of forty-five she'd retired from her managerial job due to a faulty office chair mishap and now she lied in wait for her next scandal-flavored prey.

Grandma had been so excited about our lunch date. I'd picked her up early—no sense in suffering the scorn of my aunts believing I'd left her standing alone outside the house. Her soft, light brown eyes perked up the moment she saw me. She wore her favorite outfit: a floral dress with knee-high brown stockings. Warm kisses and hugs came first, and then we set out for our meal. The diner, with its over-the-top light-green color scheme and country music, wasn't too packed. This place also met my obsessive-compulsive disorder's requirements in terms of cleanliness. I had yet to see a dirty table and the glasses stacked near the soda fountain were spotless. Even the staff worked like this was a clean-up site for radioactive waste.

We slid into a booth and waited for our server.

"How have you been, Natalya?" Grandma asked me in Russian while I wiped off the table with baby wipes. Might as well give into temptation and clean again.

"Good. I've been working overtime at the flea market, but we've got a few new college students to break in. If I can't get them in line, I might have to go alpha on them."

Grandma chuckled. "Are they werewolves?"

"No." I sighed, spotting a head turning to look our way in a booth near ours. "That's the problem."

Our server showed up, so we switched to English. Pearl had been working here since I was a pup. Time hadn't affected her charm. The little, old lady was about as tall as Grandma, but she had spunk.

"What can I get for you two young ladies?" she asked with a smile.

I opened my menu, trying to ignore the fine hairs prickling on the back of my neck when I felt like someone observed me. Grandma glanced at her menu. She touched the pictures, going from page to page.

"Two warm cups of tea to start, please," I began. "Grandma, what would you like?"

"This, please," she said with a heavy accent as she pointed to the Reuben sandwich.

"Sound great, honey." The server didn't miss a beat. "What else?"

I chuckled. Pearl knew we came for a real meal. "Eat whatever you want, Grandma."

Grandma pointed to two other sandwich platters: a grilled cheese deluxe and a pastrami with all the fixings.

"You packin' a lunch for home?" Pearl jested.

"Sure..." I ordered two burgers cooked to the point of charred carbon, piping hot fries, and a pork chop sandwich. I would've loved some fruit, but my trust only went so far. "That's all for here. What I don't eat I'll take ... *home*."

Pearl finished her mad scribbling. "Well, it's good to see women not holding back healthy appetites. Let me get you those two cups of tea."

The moment our server left, the blonde watching us turned back to her food. The bowl of soup in front of Renissa no longer had steam, but her Coke—which even I could smell from here—was full. Her barely there black eyebrows were too high on her forehead and her red lips pursed as if deep in thought.

Grandma sparked another conversation in Russian about a familiar topic: my brother and her need for him to produce more grandbabies. He already had a daughter the Stravinskys spoiled rotten.

I, on the other hand, had yet to get knocked up. Maybe my lady parts were on strike.

"I don't know why his wife isn't pregnant again," Grandma began. "He's young. His wife isn't even one hundred years old yet ..."

My eyebrow rose. "Grandma, I think you're mixing Karey up with one of her wood nymph sisters. I think she's going on thirty—not a century."

Having woodland creatures for in-laws made the most interesting family dinners. Especially when Aunt Vera pulled out the roasted deer.

"But she's still young. I was having babies right up until my Pyotr died. Knowing him, he'd have found a way to have me swollen with pups from the grave." Now the conversation was going in a weird direction, so I was thankful when two servers appeared with all the food.

The busboy paused for a moment. *Nope, we weren't waiting for more friends to show up.*

By the time all our plates were placed, there wasn't room for much else. The glow in Grandma's eyes was worth it. Delicately, she unfolded her paper napkin and placed it in her lap. She grabbed the grilled cheese sandwich first. Less than a minute later, not a single crumb remained. Real teeth made chowing down so much faster than the dentures some of the older wolves wore.

Pearl returned to check on us. "I can see your grandma was hungry. It's good to see you making sure your grandma still gets out."

"She does sometimes," I replied. "She prefers to keep to herself." My *babushka* had the patience of a saint, but dumb humans irked her every once in a while.

Grandma continued to eat, oblivious to most of our conversation since her English wasn't that good.

Pearl added water to our glasses. "Have you ever considered taking her to the senior center? My uncle goes there, and he's made so many friends. He's even got a girlfriend." She giggled. "You got a man, Mrs. Lasovskaya?"

Grandma looked up and smiled. "No husband," she murmured in her soft voice. "Widow."

"You don't have to stay that way," Pearl said. "I bet the right man is looking for you!" She then went on about seniors having virtual Facebook parties, hooking up through websites, and such. As if that was what the hip and happening retirees were doing.

With those words, Grandma gave me a small smile. That bless-her-little-human-heart look.

Renissa's head turned our way again. I tried to return her open stare with a bit of a glare, but even most werewolves didn't find me intimidating. A growl under my breath usually sufficed, too. Unfortunately, from where she sat she wouldn't hear that shit either.

I could practically see the hamster wheel turning in Renissa's head. *Lasovskaya matriarch on the prowl, wives hide your husbands!*

By the time we finished our meals—all of it—Renissa still hadn't eaten her food, but I had a sinking suspicion she'd had her fill of something much tastier.

Two days later, I was at my parents' house eating an early dinner in the late afternoon. I hadn't invited myself over, I just showed up to eat, especially since my mate, Thorn Grantham, was out of town handling pack business.

My mom had worked all day and hadn't cooked any food, but one thing was certain in the Stravinsky household: leftovers could be procured in any corner. Whether it was the freshly baked bread, the *rogaliki* pastries from breakfast, or the roasted lamb from yesterday, food was readily available to warm up.

I was relaxing in the living room with Grandma and Aunt Olga, who is Grandma's caretaker during the day.

Mom and Dad had yet to come home from work—which meant I gobbled up good food while Grandma and Aunt Olga watched Russian television. Instead of the old, loud tapes they loved to watch all the damn time, I finally hooked them up with a Russian channel through satellite TV. With pride, I turned on TVCI.

As to why my parents hadn't done it yet, I didn't know. I

guess it was much more nostalgic watching VHS-taped shows from their generation.

A variety show was on and couples competed for a vacation in the Baltics. Apparently, all they had to do was embarrass themselves singing badly to their significant other. The audience voted for the winner. One guy crooned like a howling monkey about to fling shit at people. I about choked on my food laughing my ass off. When I turned to look at my relatives, their straight faces said their disapproval in my taste of shows.

With a sigh, I switched back to the VHS tape. A show that they'd seen over fifty million times was better than watching something completely brand new.

I mean, who wouldn't want to watch some dude try to make his lady happy?

The doorbell rang, which I took as a sign from heaven to get a break from watching a show I'd seen before. On the way to the door, I caught our visitor's scent. It was just another human, but the subtle aftershave, a rather nice one with a hint of black pepper and spice, tickled my nose.

I peeked through the hole and saw a dapper elderly man clad in gray trousers, a dark blue vest, and a baseball cap.

I opened the door. Maybe he was selling tickets for the Shriners. I didn't mind those visits.

"Good afternoon, I'm Carlson McGraw," he said crisply. He took off his cap. "Is Svetlana home?"

"Huh?" My mouth opened then dropped.

A car pulled up and a second elderly man—this one bearing flowers—climbed out. I couldn't stop myself from laughing aloud. That busybody Renissa struck again. Was that chick patrolling the senior center looking for lonely dudes?

"Svetlana who?" I peeked over my shoulder. Aunt Olga stood and walked toward the door.

"What is it?" she mouthed in Russian.

"Gentleman callers for Grandma," I replied in Russian.

"What?" Her reply in English pretty much reflected how amused she was. Like any demure woman who had beauty queen experience, she touched her hair and straightened her shirt. The woman never left the house looking unpresentable, but that's the way she was.

"Please come in." I couldn't resist. This was much more interesting than any TV show.

I gave them five minutes with our pack before they'd be shuffling away screaming.

Carlson nodded to Aunt Olga on the way in. I was about to close the door when I noticed the second guy had reached our sidewalk.

I took a step toward the stairs, but he waved me away. "Almost there. I'm coming, Svetlana."

I bit back a chuckle. Did Grandma even know these guys?

"Grandma," I asked her in Russian, "what have you been doing during your outings?"

Instead of shrugging—like I expected her to, she'd adjusted her brown stockings and the scarf covering her head. Was she seriously primping herself?

Her brown eyes twinkled with mischief. Might as well let her have some fun.

The second guy, Gary was his name, made it up the steps and both men took a seat on the couch near Grandma. At Grandma's insistence, Aunt Olga hurried into the kitchen to prepare a service of tea along with some of Mom's scones.

The gentlemen sat silent looking at Grandma for the longest time before I spoke.

"So umm, where did you two meet my grandmother?" I asked.

"Oh, everyone at the senior center knows Svetlana," Gary said before Carlson could jump in. He'd given her a bouquet of flowers and Grandma practically beamed.

Grandma had a caretaker during the day, so when did she go there?

"In what way?" I had to know. "How often have you all talked with her?"

"Every now and then—not as often as I'd like—she visits during Bingo night." Carlson's grin was infectious. Just watching these two guys, one with a cane who barely made it up the driveway, try to mac on my grandma was hilarious.

"She's quite feisty with those chips," Gary added.

"You don't talk to anyone, but I think that makes you more mysterious, Ms. Svetlana."

Did either of them know her English wasn't very good?

Carlson said, "One night she had five cards instead two."

Did a higher number of Bingo cards mean Grandma was a hardcore player?

Aunt Olga brought out the tea and scones. As she handed Carlson his cup, he spouted, "How lucky I am to spend some time with three pretty ladies this afternoon."

"Oh, stop it," Gary's hand tightened on his cane. "You say the same thing to the physical therapist at the center. Come up with some new material."

Carlson grated back. "I made it up the driveway. Is your performance guaranteed?"

I hesitated eating my next bite for fear of choking from laughter.

Carlson continued. "If you're interested, Svetlana, Bingo night is coming up again. I'd be happy if you and I could sit next to each other."

Heh, heh. Grandma just got asked on a date. Nice.

"*Bah.* What are you gonna tell the gals who like to sit next to you?" Gary asked.

"Sadly, they're gonna have to be disappointed," Carlson replied.

I glanced at Grandma who watched their exchange with amusement.

"Do you know these two?" I asked her in Russian.

"I've seen them before, but that's about it," she said.

"And they just showed up. Do they know how old you are? That their ancestors *hadn't* reached America yet when you were born?"

She chuckled. "My Nat didn't know Grandma could still bring 'em. Eh? Before my Pyotr I had plenty of gentlemen callers. All around the village, the werewolves came running—while the humans ran away. This change is rather nice."

"What is she saying?" Carlson asked with a toothy grin. "She's so soft-spoken."

"She remembers you two from the senior center," I lied. "Who wouldn't miss two handsome young fellows like yourselves?"

Gary took a bit of scone and had to quickly adjust his upper denture. Mom did make her cookies a bit harder than most. Once he got his teeth back in his mouth, he spoke. "If you're not going to Bingo on Saturday, we could always go out for a chicken dinner at the place off Main Street. I can pick you up around four o'clock."

Carlson wasn't about to let his friend ruin his chances.

"You're not picking anybody up. Your fifty-year-old *ex*-wife dropped you off here."

Ouch. Now that was an equivalent of a low-blow. Too bad he liked 'em young.

Gary grunted. "And how long did it take you to get here? We passed you going twenty in a twenty-five mile per hour zone."

"I happen to be safe," Carlson spouted. "Since I *drive* a car I enjoy that privilege."

"You and your piece of shit—I mean, crap—Lincoln Crestliner barely made it here, too. Did Ford pull that off the assembly line back in the 20s?"

The wolf in me, usually gleeful with the prospects of a fight, didn't expect much. Maybe shoving at some point. Things were about to get heated—if you could say that—when the doorbell rang again. Aunt Olga didn't bother to get up. She was far too busy enjoying the impending scuffle.

"Natalya," Grandma said with a strange tilt to her head, "Answer the door, *devushka*." She ignored the two men already vying for her affection and her attention was on the new arrival. If she hadn't used the endearment, I wouldn't have bothered.

So I became the doorman yet again. Who would it be this time? Another senior center dude on the prowl? Somebody's elderly dad looking for a Russian hottie? This time, on the way to the door, a new scent hit my nose. One I hadn't smelled in a long time. Sulphur with a tinge of rusted iron. A tightness bit into my chest.

Did I dare look? I paused before peeking through the peephole. All I saw was the top of a dark green hat. Whoever was standing there tilted their head forward to obscure their face.

My hand rested on the doorknob. Should I ask who it was first? Only a fool invited trouble across their doorstep.

But Grandma had told me to open the door, so I complied.

The hat slowly rose, revealing a brown-eyed, olive-skinned gentleman with wrinkles all over his face. Most of them vanished when his lips stretched out into an unsettling grin.

"I'd like to call on Miss Svetlana," he said crisply.

CHAPTER 3

Now most folks, those who still carried around their common sense in their back pockets, would've lied to weird-smelling strangers and shut the door.

The wolf in me whined. Tingles of dark magic raced up my fingertips and bit into my palms.

This guy wasn't from the senior center.

The new arrival, who stood no higher than my shoulders, walked smoothly into the living room. Compared to the other two dressed in their casual Sunday best, this gentleman had on a garish dark green suit. The pants were too big while the suitcoat looked tailored to fit his lanky frame.

"You two," he said to the guys without missing a beat. "Out."

Right in the middle of arguing, the two men stopped and stiffly rose.

What the hell was going on here? At a time like this, I wished I had my goblin knife. I'd stowed it away in the back of my car. The last time I'd put it into my purse it had turned into a battle-axe. I had nothing left but tattered leather.

"Grandma," I whispered. If something happened, she'd never outrun him. Yet I'd been wrong to underestimate her before. When the Long Island Pack cornered me, my grandmother protected me using werewolf magic.

Her hand rose to silence me. Her face, which only held the hint of a smile, didn't reveal much else. Sweet Svetlana was gone.

It took a while for Gary and Carlson to leave the house, but leave they did. Before I shut the door, I caught Gary on his cellphone talking to his ex-wife. "Come pick me up, Betty ..."

On the other side of the room, our new visitor had taken a seat on the La-Z-Boy Dad usually claimed. He wasn't interested in the warmed up cushions near Grandma. I sat there instead.

Briefly, he glanced at me and offered me that unsettling smile of his. "Good afternoon, Svetlana," he said in crystal clear Russian. "Long time no see."

Aunt Olga stiffened. Even she knew this guy smelled weird.

"Philip Divine. This is an *unexpected* pleasure," Grandma replied in Russian.

My gaze flicked from Philip to Grandma. Then back again.

"All this time I thought you were lying low," he whispered. "But I overheard you might be open to meeting people again."

Renissa Delaney-Danford. Was she putting up fliers in hell or something?

Grandma harrumphed. "Philip, you're the last person I'd expect to believe in rumors."

His grin somehow widened. "In every rumor, there's often a grain of truth."

She snorted then turned to Olga. "Go for a short walk."

Aunt Olga looked to me as if she expected me to protest. I shrugged.

"Mama?" Aunt Olga implored.

"Now."

I'd never seen my aunt move as fast as she did to scamper out of the house. Once the door slammed shut, Grandma leaned forward. "How long did it take you to follow me this time?"

Follow? This shit was getting weirder and weirder.

"How much time doesn't matter." He placed his long fingers over his knees. "What matters is you and I may have the dinner we missed out on all those years ago."

Grandma's eyebrows rose. "The last dinner didn't go as well, Philip."

"Can't a man have a second chance? I see you've opened your home to those bags of bones."

"You caught me at a vulnerable time back then."

He nodded. "Pyotr had gone to the great woods for his final rest while my pretty Svetlana sat all alone with children. It was a perfect time for companionship."

"Not your kind," she bit out. "Like I'd sleep with you after your sorry, little serenade."

Questions rested on my lips, but I didn't dare speak. Had she really known him since Grandpa died centuries ago in the 1600s?

"One dinner with me won't change a thing."

"That's what you said in Minsk."

"Aren't you curious to see what would happen?" His fingers twitched, and my eyes focused on the way his fingers resembled spider's legs. He sucked in a deep breath. "Your perfume has changed over the years. Back in Russia, you smelled like the spring, practically full of new life. Now there is an underlying musk that I find rather attractive. You've touched the shadows."

This shit had grown from slightly odd to beyond weird now. I inhaled a scone to stop the nervous sparks in my stomach.

Grandma crossed her arms, and a pensive look flashed over her face. For a brief moment, I caught a hint of her youth, the purse of her thin lips, the way she tapped her foot as if unnerved or impatient.

"What I've done over the years doesn't involve you, Philip."

He laughed softly. "What would one dinner cost you? We could eat at this nice Italian restaurant called Roger's Place."

I immediately flinched. Roger's Place was where I had an unfortunate date with a fellow employee that hadn't ended well. His zombie minion showed up to serve us our dinner since his waiter wasn't worthy.

"Uh, how about Jake's Burgers?" I intervened. "The place is really clean and the food is totally sanitary—"

"Do you seriously think I'd take my Svetlana to that dump?" Philip cut me off.

My mouth snapped shut. Roger's Place wasn't much fancier. This was a small town after all. If he really wanted to impress her, he should offer to take her to NYC or Atlantic City, but then again, why was I even trying to communicate with a creature I had yet to identify?

"One dinner," she said. "At Roger's Place. Tonight."

"Wha?" I mumbled.

"Splendid." He stood without making a sound. "I look forward to our tête-á-tête."

"I'm sure."

The moment Philip walked out the door I stood to go after him.

"Sit down, Natalya."

I gawked at my grandmother. "Are you seriously going out on a date with that *thing*?"

"Yes, I am."

"Are you that lonely—"

"Sometimes."

I took the free seat next to her on the couch. "All this time, you've never been with someone else. I just find it hard to believe you'd—"

"Accept time with another man?"

"Accept time with a *creature* that smells like death smeared on a shoe!"

She chuckled and reached over to cup my cheeks. "There are many things you still have to learn and one of them is about sacrifices. As much as I can never replace Pyotr, I must be the one to open myself up to enjoy companionship if I need it."

"But what about Bingo night?"

"Bingo night with those humans?" She snorted. "None of them would know what to do with me."

"And that thing would?"

Grandma rose from the seat, ignoring my question. "I'm going to take a nap before my date." She even *giggled*. "Tell your aunt I'm fine."

Fine? Grandma had jumped off the edge of the deep end of the pool, and I didn't know if she could swim, let alone if I could save her.

CHAPTER 4

Two hours later, I still hadn't left the house. Matter of fact, I'd camped out on the steps of my parents' home with my goblin knife. I'd acquired the weapon from a tricky goblin while trying to save my brother. I waited patiently with the knife tucked behind my back for that creature to show up to get Grandma.

Soon enough, the blade would reveal what I dealt with. Maybe it would turn into a spear or something. I laughed a bit. It had been a while since I'd hunted.

Time passed, and no one came to the front of the house. Six P.M. came and went. By quarter after, my heart fell a bit. Was my grandma stood up by that creepy asshole?

I marched into the place, ready to rant, when I noticed only Mom and Dad sat at the kitchen table.

"Where's Grandma?"

"She went out the back door not too long ago," Mom replied. "Said she was heading out to meet with a friend."

That tricky old lady got me good.

"And you just let her go?" I gasped.

Mom didn't bother hiding her amusement. "You must think my mama is *fragile*."

"She is! Have you seen how long it takes her to put on her stockings?"

Mom shook her head. "She'll be fine, Nat. She looked nice and everything. Truth be told," Mom's voice lowered, "She put on my red lipstick. Dark red, I tell you. I bet Mama's gonna get *lucky* tonight."

Horror smacked me hard against the face. I shuffled backwards and headed for the door. On the way out, I caught a few of their words.

"What's wrong with her?" Mom asked Dad.

"She's close to her *babushka*. Natalya's never seen her with anyone before."

With anyone? I raced down the steps and jumped into my Nissan Altima. Gee, what could happen if the date went wrong? That creature might well gobble up Grandma, and I wasn't having that.

I made it to downtown South Toms River in record time. For a small town, we didn't have many stoplights to get in the way. During the whole drive, my hand clutched the steering wheel while the other one squeezed the hilt on the goblin knife hard enough to hurt.

The parking lot for Roger's Place wasn't too packed, so I found a spot toward the back. Might as well try to be inconspicuous. Once in the lobby, I peered inside and hoped I wouldn't be spotted. The wondrous scents of baked spaghetti and chicken scampi reached my nose. The fact I hadn't eaten dinner hit my stomach.

"Hey, Nat," a lady who often shopped at The Bend of the River Flea Market where I worked waved.

"Hello," I whispered softly.

At the other side of the room, about a table away from

the spot where I'd had my disastrous date with Quinton the janitor, Grandma sat across from Philip Divine. Like Mom had said, Grandma dolled herself up. I stood there transfixed—before I pushed myself into action and hurried to a spot near the bar. With my back to Grandma, I couldn't see them, but she was vivid in my mind.

Her scarf had been left at home. Soft, white hair fell in waves to her waist. Her thin lips were glossy from red lipstick. A bit of pink blush made her cheeks rosy.

Grandma looked absolutely ethereal.

The bartender approached me, but after a brief shake of my head, he sauntered off. Time to listen in. Tuning out the other sounds in the dining room required focus, but I'd eavesdropped on enough conversations to get pretty good. And well, not too many people in South Toms River spoke Russian. Catching the soft lilt to Grandma's voice was easy.

"You might want to get down to business, but I happen to be hungry," Grandma said.

What business?

I hated coming in after a conversation began.

"Oh, get anything you like, then. I heard the lasagna is to *die* for here," Philip replied.

I shuddered, recalling how Quinton's undead minion waltzed up to us, spouting how our human server—the poor boy—was unworthy to serve his master. Just thinking about the minion's decaying smell pushed my anxiety to alarming levels. My stomach muscles clenched and the air rushing into my lungs stopped for a moment. I sucked in a deep breath and closed my eyes.

Focus, Nat.

A server, this one with a pulse, showed up and took their order. I waited patiently. The bartender wandered over again, so I ordered a citrus martini. My first choice had been water, but then I caught the impatient glint in his eye.

"How long are you going to follow me?" Grandma asked Philip, a hint of exasperation in her voice.

"As long as we've known each other, Sveta, you shouldn't be surprised to see me."

"I kind of hoped you perished in Moscow during that fire in 1812."

Philip scoffed. "Napoleon's troops coming in for a little visit wouldn't keep me away."

She made a rude noise as I took a sip of my drink. "Your persistence isn't attractive. If people knew what you really are—"

"They'd tremble in fear?" he finished coldly.

"Trembling wasn't what I had in mind." I caught her hard swallow over the clink of silverware. "Humans avoid you, and normally, werewolves do as well, but you preyed on me at a point in my life when I was lonely."

He laughed. "A lonely, budding werewolf who knows old magic, a meal fit for any king who dwells in darkness."

My mind kicked over again and again. *Why can't I figure out what Philip Divine is?* The goblin blade sat lifeless in my purse—not a good sign. Did that mean I dealt with a goblin of some kind?

Philip also knew about her knowledge of old magic. Not too long ago, I didn't even know werewolves could cast spells. It's rather mind-blowing. Werewolves called it old magic, and these days, the laws governing werewolves, called the Code, prohibited any werewolf from using it.

"I'm not what I used to be. I've got too many years on me to play with old magic," she replied.

Their food arrived, and I had to wait before Philip spoke again. Oh, man, I could practically smell their platters of veal parmigiana from over here. At least they hadn't ordered the lasagna.

Grandma ate in agonizingly slow bites, rare for her, while Philip ordered for their check and stopped making noise after a few minutes. Had he even bothered to eat?

Their server brought their check. Alarm crept down my back.

"Power seeps from you, my dear," Philip said. "No, it isn't as strong anymore, but you're more than what I need. You've always been." The sounds of his chair scraping back stung my ears.

I turned slightly to peek over my shoulder and opened my purse to reach for the lifeless weapon inside. If I had to use what equated to a letter opener on him, I would.

"Why delay what's about to happen?" he asked.

Grandma's chair moved. She stood. Did she really plan to leave with this crazy bastard? From the corner of my eye, I watched her leave her napkin on her plate.

"Every road has an ending, Svetlana Lasovskaya," Philip Divine said as they headed for the door. "Take a walk with me to see yours."

CHAPTER 5

In the time I wasted paying for my drink and running out to the parking lot, Grandma and Philip crossed Chamberlain Street and entered the woods.

They weren't going that fast. I was trailing two *old* people.

Even though I smelled them, their destination was clear: South Toms River Park.

I raced after them—narrowly avoiding evening traffic on the road. Following Grandma's scent was easy. Eventually, I caught up to them in a clearing with a single set of playground equipment. The half moon cast a radiant glow along the metal curves and lines of the jungle gym. The park benches could be barely seen among the murky shadows.

Grandma stood on one side of the clearing while Philip Divine was on the other. At first, neither of them moved in the darkness. Then a strange sensation crawled along my skin like beetles scuttling beneath a fallen log. The alarming tinges of magic building. The wolf stirring in my chest urged my feet to move backwards.

Not without Grandma...

Philip moved first.

I prepared the goblin blade for action. Any moment now, he'd be on her. *Uh, I take that back.* His walk was so wobbly it couldn't even be described as a stroll.

By the time he reached the middle of the clearing, he'd found his footing and advanced faster now, crossing the field while Grandma stood there, a slow-moving morsel waiting to be eaten.

"If Pyotr had never married you, would you have still come to me if I'd called?" he whispered, his voice as deep as an empty grave.

She made a tsk noise. "Time has never *ever* been kind to you. Even as a goblin king."

I turned to look at him. Truly look at him. Working at The Bends for so long helped me see through goblin glamour, but his magic had to be powerful. Hell, my goblin blade hadn't reacted to him at all.

I glanced at my hands. They'd be good enough to beat the crap out of him. I took a step toward the clearing, unsure what to do. I had yet to face an adversary like this one. Would I be willing to cast an old magic spell for her? Werewolves drew their power from within, an exchange of life for power. Tamara, a werewolf who had recently taught me more old magic, had given me a warning: "*The sad thing is that, as spellcasters pulling from ourselves, we have little say in where we pull from. You could be pulling from your fingertip. You could be pulling from your stomach. The worse spots are your internal organs.*"

I took another step without any doubt. *The answer was undeniably yes.*

Philip was closer now. Just a few steps away. The wrinkled, translucent skin on his cheeks was now a sickly brownish-green. His gaudy, dark green suit appeared muddied.

Spiky teeth filled his mouth and forced his jaw to jut out at a gruesome angle.

Fear catapulted into me, forcing me into a breakneck sprint toward Grandma. All the words I needed waited on the edge of my tongue. Everything Tamara had taught me about old magic. With a few words, I could set his ass on fire, freeze him into a goblin kabob, or shake the heavens until the ground opened to swallow him whole.

Grandma opened her arms. Almost as if to welcome him. Blackened claws extended from his fingertips toward her.

Almost there.

I murmured the first old magic word. *Daka.*

I stumbled but kept going. *Binu.*

The moment his claw touched her chest, she bowed inward, her face cringing.

My third word melted into a moan.

Oh, please God, no!

They fell into a heap. A screech followed by a crunch filled the clearing.

But it wasn't my *babushka.* The crackly sound—like dead leaves crushed underfoot—didn't match what I said. Grandma's chest was now a black void sucking him in.

I ground to a halt, mouth gaping in awe at the damnedest thing I'd ever seen. And I've seen really crazy shit. The crunchy noises were Philip trying to escape. Bit by bit, she pulled him in, her eyes closed while her mouth moved as if murmuring a prayer.

The smell of ozone was overwhelming now. Bitter enough to coat my tongue and suffocate me where I stood.

One moment Philip Divine was there, and in the next with a single wet slurp, Grandma Lasovskaya swallowed him whole. I turned away from the sight.

When I glanced back at her, my mouth still hung open, stunned.

"Grandma?" I whispered.

The moonlight didn't shine down on an old woman, but someone my age.

She placed her index finger against a perfectly curved mouth. Beautiful blonde hair, instead of white, framed an oval face with shining brown eyes. I couldn't help but return the devilish grin she gave me.

Was that a dimple I saw in her cheek?

She placed her fingertip on my mouth to hush me from asking more questions.

"Let's go home, Nat," she implored as she took my hand, and what a wonderful hand she had. What had once been fragile, papery skin was firm to the touch.

We reached the edge of the woods on Chamberlain. Instead of heading for the parking lot for Roger's Place, she tugged me to walk down the road. So many questions circled my head. First of all, *how in the hell was I gonna explain this to Mom and Dad?*

"Just for a little while," she said.

As we continued down the road, I began to understand why. The wind played with her hair, but with each step we took, the blonde faded to white. Her confident step slowed to a steady shuffle. Time took its rightful place behind us. The firm hold of her grip weakened. By the time we reached my parents' Colonial home, I held my elderly Grandma's hand.

Before we climbed up the porch steps, I had to know what went on before she escaped me.

"What happened back there, Grandma?" I tugged her to stay outside for a bit.

"Eh, I threw away some dead weight, and now I'm rid of

Philip Divine for good." She was so casual about it. Like it was a break up or something.

I groaned. "You can't do all *that* and expect me not to ask questions."

Her laugh was sweet, a welcome sound to my ears. "Do you remember the first time you saw me change form?"

I'd never forget the night she saved me from invading pack members who wanted to kill my injured brother while he slept. She'd used old magic and transformed into a hideous creature with great strength. Her sacrifice had left her sleeping for days.

"A part of my life was taken away that night." Her grin returned. "I took that back tonight."

"How?" Now she had my attention.

"Bah! Like I'd tell you how I manipulate dark goblin magic!" She gave me a gentle shove. "Your goblin boss doesn't even play with that mess and neither should you."

Exasperated, I continued to follow her to the house steps. Yet again, Grandma's many secrets had come to light.

"Okay, how about a hint?" I asked.

"*Nyet.*"

"Stop being greedy, Grandma!"

"Ha, so funny. The *hoarder* is telling me not to be greedy."

For the longest time, I'd called myself a collector instead of a hoarder, but thanks to therapy, I could see mere semantics hadn't made my problems go away. Grandma's words were in jest. "Fine. I hope you enjoyed your little *date*, then."

"Of course, I did. A *devuskha* like me has to play the field. Get the boys jealous." She chuckled, and I couldn't shake that she might've lost her natural mind.

"Would you like me to stay with you tonight?" I

managed as Mom opened the door. Mom must've heard us coming.

"Nah. I'm feeling spry this evening. I might even be up for a friendly game of Bingo with Carlson on Saturday." She winked at me.

"Who knows," she added. "With all those men calling on me, I might win more than fifty bucks."

The End

CURSED

CHAPTER 1

Reader's Note: This story takes place one year after
Compelled (Coveted #3)

THE BROCHURE quite loosely used the words "quaint Southern charm" about Bright Haven, Georgia. I turned the trifold piece of paper upside-down just in case I missed a disclaimer on the advertisement. Before we stopped for gas on the outskirts of town, we'd passed a kudzu-covered, lopsided *Welcome to Bright Haven* sign and two abandoned bungalows.

My husband, Thorn Grantham, gave me a wry grin as he pumped gas into our SUV. "Natalya, stop worrying."

Worrying? *Pfft.* I was a werewolf. My vision worked just fine, and based on what I saw as we drove into town, there was little to excite me. The 800-mile trip from Jersey to eastern Georgia should be the beautiful wedding we never had when we became mates a year ago. A chance for us to experience saying our marriage vows in a more formal setting.

Once he finished filling up the SUV, he got in and leaned over to kiss my forehead. His warm lips left an impression on my heart, too. His sandalwood scent filled my senses, and I couldn't resist smiling. He always knew what to say at the right times.

"You'll be fine," he said softly. "We'll be fine. They promised us our renewal vows would be an event to remember."

I needed something good to remember. On the night we became mates for life, I had to fight my way into our pack and prove my place as alpha female. Now that we were together, I wanted so much more with Thorn, but at a pace I could manage. A family someday, maybe even a chance to feel normal. For the past couple of months, he noticed I hadn't felt the same about kids.

The need to be optimistic tugged at me. A rather hard task when I was a professional worrier. A few weeks ago, Thorn received an invitation from a pack alpha who briefly stopped in South Toms River. The invite included a weekend stay at a romantic Southern bed and breakfast. For someone like me who wasn't fond of staying in strange place, I wasn't keen on the idea—until Thorn gave me the brochure. The place was an antiquarian's paradise with over ten antique shops. Like an antique junkie waiting for her next fix, I immediately packed our bags—while leaving plenty of space for whatever goodies we planned to bring home.

So now that we drove down Main Street deeper into town, where the Uncle Barker's Bed and Breakfast was located, I wondered if maybe there was a misprint on the brochure and maybe this pamphlet was for another town. Grand, live oak trees along the street blocked most of the overcast, November sky. Water from a recent rain shower dripped down the Spanish moss hanging from the trees. Those things I expected. What made me wary were the boarded up shop windows and the cars with flat tires along the curbs. There weren't many people walking around either. Only a lone woman in a long overcoat walked her dog, her face obscured by the dark blue scarf on her head. Something about her slow gait pulled me in to stare.

The narrow street opened to reveal the center of town and a glorious stone building surrounded by trees. I leaned against the window to look closer. Columns of dark red and white bricks peeked from between tall pines and cypress trees. As more of it became visible, I noticed there wasn't much to see—what was left of the building was nothing more than old, charred wood and stone collapsing on itself from time. A part of me wanted to explore the land as a wolf. To see and smell what lay hidden from human eyes, but the human side of me didn't want to touch the emptiness that lingered.

"Is that what's left of the old Bright Haven Fortress?" Thorn asked.

"Yeah." I wiped off the fog accumulating from my breath on the window. "According to the brochure, it was burned down and rebuilt three times. Once by the British, then the Union Army, and the third time was an accidental fire from the drunken mayor during a Fourth of July celebration in the 1920s."

"I guess the town was determined to keep the place," he replied. "Talk about bad luck for the place. Wow."

Not far from the fort, we pulled up to our destination. The red and green glow from Uncle Barker's Bed and Breakfast sign lit the interior of the car. I opened the door, and a gust of wind brought humidity into the car.

With a nod of approval I said, "Now this is what I call Southern charm."

Compared to the other homes we passed, the expansive three-story structure looked like Santa's sleigh crashed into the side of the house and the cheerful contents from his bag were discarded everywhere. A grin filled my face. Christmas lights covered every curved corner on the yellow and lime green house. There were still a few weeks until the Christmas holiday, but these folks knew how to throw on some cheer. The huge wreath on the door practically beckoned us to knock and sing carols.

And yet—there was more—an abundance of jigsaw-like architectural details that fit together like the white arcs over the white railings on each floor. The century-old batten, or vertically placed siding, used to build this house whispered its age to me based on the cracks in the paint and size of the single live oak in the tiny front yard. This was the kind of home I wouldn't mind living in as Thorn and I grew old. We were only in our early twenties, but I was drawn to these types of places. They had history. Someone loved this house enough repair the growing flaws over the decades.

With a skip in my step, I opened the slick, wrought-iron gate. My mate caught up with me by the time I swung my arm to knock—only to have a man open the door before I could.

Arm in mid-air, I stared at him with wide eyes and he did the same, perhaps flabbergasted that both of us surprised each other. His large brown eyes blinked a few times before a smile broke out on his face. "You must be, Mrs. Grantham," he said with exuberance. His barreled chest gave him a deep, smooth accent. "I spoke with your husband on the phone. I'm Jackson Cason, the mayor of Bright Haven."

"Call me, Natalya, please." I extended my hand, and the older werewolf shook it. I almost repeated his name, but something told me I'd stumble over it. I mouthed the name and verified the double "son."

He nodded and smiled, his mouth hard to see with such a bushy blonde mustache and beard. The mayor had the strangest, expansive eyes, like two bronze coins reflecting in the dim light of the foyer. The enticing smell of freshly baked cookies and coffee drew me to look away.

"This is a nice place you got here," Thorn said first.

"Thank you," Jackson replied. "Our pack is pleased you came at such short notice."

Thorn shrugged. "My mate and I have had a hard year. The opportunity to relax and enjoy the time here was welcomed." He glanced at me from the corner of his blue eyes and I couldn't help grinning.

"You're right on time," Jackson said with a hearty laugh.

Thorn glanced at me again. "Again. My wife."

"Our pack leader is already here. His wife wanted to prepare our meal." The older man shrugged. "Something about how my food tastes like I'd wrangled up a half-dead croc and served its head on a plate."

"I'm sure you do just fine," I said to be polite.

The outside of the house was grand, but the inside hadn't seen a broom or a duster. A layer of dust covered an ornate china hutch that extended across the wall. Tarnished silver plates and dusty Wedgwood china filled every shelf. My heart broke to see them in such poor shape.

The Friday evening shadows in the room grew longer as the faint light from outside darkened, and shortly, hard rain beat against the windows.

"We got in just in time," I managed over the rumble of thunder.

"This nasty November weather has gotten worse lately," Jackson gestured for us to follow him into the dining room. A lone, dark-haired man sat at the head of the long table covered with a white tablecloth. He sat with a straight back, his chin jutting as his sharp iron-gray eyes accessing every move we made. His scent was strong from even the doorway, leaning against us as he projected his place within his pack. This was the local alpha. The tiny hairs on the back of my neck prickled, but I ignored the feeling as Thorn rested his hand on my hip and pushed me toward a seat not far from the alpha.

"Natalya and Thorn, I'd like for you to meet our pack alpha, Calvin Braxton Cunningham. Most of the boys around town call him Cal."

Calvin cocked a grin, revealing the hint of an incisor. "Thanks for coming, Grantham." His low timbre voice was southern-smooth like a double shot of Kentucky bourbon.

My mate nodded, his gaze never leaving Calvin's as he pulled back my seat for me. They stared at each other for a moment like werewolf males always did. A dance of sorts where they virtually circled each other to sniff out their vulnerabilities. Thorn did this countless of times in front of me, but today just seeing them engaged in the staring match made Calvin seem like a deadly lionfish. The fish had an enigmatic beauty, but it underneath its colorful scales a predator swam in the dark waters hunting for the next prey. The alpha's eyebrows lowered and his smirk stretched his prominent cheeks. He didn't need cologne with all the cockiness he exuded.

Neither of them looked away, but Calvin spoke first. "How was the drive?"

"Uneventful. Just the way I like it," Thorn said smoothly.

"Good." The mayor brought in a bottle of scotch with a few shot glasses. "Let's get this dinner started before Mary Ann brings out the food, shall we?"

Twenty minutes later, we were all gathered together and surrounded by delicious food. Mary Ann, the pack's alpha female, was a sharp-tongued redhead with ruddy skin. She marched out tray after tray of steaming delights: a bowl of green bean casserole, steaming corn bread, fried chicken, and sweet potato pie.

"And that's just the first round," she boasted.

She knew how to keep hungry werewolves satisfied.

Thorn and I dug into the eating fest, not holding back from the generous servings.

Mary Ann tried to pour me another drink with a smile, but I declined.

"Just one." I rarely drank. As much I liked to have fun, having my wits about me was much more preferred. Especially with a man like Cal around. He kept drinking and couldn't keep his mouth shut.

"Have you ever been down here before?" he asked Thorn.

"Not really. I've stuck to the northeast. This year has been different though," he glanced briefly at me with a smile. "But due to pack problems, I've stayed close to home. Now that things are stable, I've enjoyed traveling more."

"This town has run into hard times recently, but back in my time, it was in its glory."

"Here we go ..." His wife rolled her eyes and tried to give him another serving of pie, but he pushed it away.

Calvin poured Thorn another shot of scotch. "Oh, hush, woman." He tipped back his own drink in a single swallow and then kept talking. His voice showed not a single sign that the liquor touched his senses. "This year, I'll be one hundred and seventy-five years old. If I'd been born a year or two sooner, I'd have a leg up on the 'ole mayor here."

Jackson nodded. "You're still a crusty old fart in my eyes, boy."

Fulton continued. "Back then, this land had been different. All the electronics and gadgets we have today have painted the landscape into something I don't recognize anymore. I miss the good ole' days. I'm assuming you haven't explored all the sights around here. You ever been to a plantation before?"

Thorn shook his head.

"You such see one if you get the chance. Over the years, they've gotten a bad rep due to Southern *traditions*. But they hold good memories for some." Calvin appeared wistful. "Even during wartime."

"So you were a soldier?"

"I'm still a soldier, Grantham. There will always be an enemy to face." He stared at us. I squirmed in my seat until Thorn took my hand under the table. "My first real taste of fighting was in General Sherman's March to Sea back in 1864." His long fingers played with the rim of his shot glass. "My regiment was on their way to offer reinforcements to Fort McAllister, but we never made it. Those Yankees burned countless homes and plantations." Then his fingers froze and he gripped the glass tight enough for his knuckles to turn white. "After that, we didn't have access to hardly any food for my brothers in arms. We had to *take* what we needed."

"And how did you do that?" I asked. I had a feeling he didn't buy what he needed from peddlers by the side of the road.

His sneer was prickly. "There was this plantation near

Savannah that was fortified by the Yankees. I was more than happy to join a few other hungry boys. Like I said, we took what we needed from them. Food ... and otherwise."

Thorn's grip tightened until my hand ached. Lightning flashed outside the windows, and my shoulders tensed as thunder boomed to shake the house, even the dinner plates on the table.

Calvin continued his tale. "Once or twice, I ran into slaves stealing away from other plantations. Once I caught this old woman trying to run away. She had the nerve to put up a fight, too. What I remember the most about her was what she tried to take with her—this strange statue made from some kind of wood I'd never seen before. She kept saying she needed to protect it. To bury it to keep it from the likes of men like me. A bunch of hogwash. I took it from her—she didn't need something so valuable—but her eyes had been fierce, like she had a fire inside her that a man like me couldn't extinguish."

"What did you do to her?" I murmured.

"What do you think happened to her?" He let his final words hang in the air.

I wanted to say that he probably killed her and stole for himself that strange statue she'd had. I wanted to stay that he probably returned home a hero without worrying about the stain of what he'd done on his fingers or his conscience. Yet when I opened my mouth I realized I didn't want to say anything at all.

"Well, you might've fought with those Johnny Rebels, but it's a good thing we hadn't met in the field, 'cause I would've shot your crazy ass down," Jackson said with a laugh and licked his fingers. What was left of his fried chicken was nothing but naked bones.

Calvin joined his laughter. "You were a lot skinnier in those days, friend. You could've taken me."

"Mmm-hmm. I would've whipped your ass good."

The joviality lifted the somber mood at the table. I tried to smile at Thorn. Calvin was just the alpha of these parts, after all. We were here for us and not for him.

CHAPTER 2

The next morning, I took my time waking up. Tonight was the full moon, after all. Every sense escalated to dizzying heights. Safe in the dim lights of our second-story room, the rain continued with a dull cadence outside, bringing with it wind. The light taps from a branch beat against the window over our bed, its shape casting ghostly shadows on the walls. We had the largest suite to ourselves.

I curled up next to Thorn and rest my head against his back. He smelled so good, but during the full moon, most werewolves smelled like tantalizing pre-packaged sex. Thorn was no different.

He rolled over until he leaned over me. "Up already? I bet you spent the night with dreams of old dusty vases and vintage Christmas ornaments, didn't you?"

"Not really." *Yes, I had.*

His hands slipped down my sides, and he lowered his head for a long kiss. "We could stay here in bed. And get ready for tonight."

His lips rained kisses along the nape of my neck, his breath soft against my skin.

"I want you," he whispered.

My body hummed every time he said those words. Over a year ago, our relationship had been tumultuous since he was forced into an engagement with another woman, but now he was mine. He rolled over on top of me, the evidence of his arousal pressing into my thigh. His black boxer shorts did little to hide that.

His lips trailed to my chin until he met my mouth. Kissing Thorn was like dreaming of paradise and then experiencing everything there: his mouth was sunshine, his hands on my skin cool ocean waters, his caress like a never-ending sunset. As our kiss deepened, his warm hands snuck under my shirt, kneading my skin until he cupped my breast.

A moan escaped my mouth into his.

"Mine," he said against my mouth. "I want to claim you as mine again and again tonight." He urgently tasted my lips as his fingers trailed down to between us. His fingertips brushed against my heat, and my body trembled betraying my need for control.

"There are so many things I want to do to you after we hunt." He gave me a wicked grin. "Don't even think about sleeping."

He tried to pull up my shirt, but I tugged it back down. He knew what having sex right now meant. No matter how hard it would be to say no to Thorn today, he had to understand how I felt about starting a family.

"How about we wait until tonight?" I suggested, but he knew what I meant. I was brushing him off yet again.

He sighed. "My hand is getting tired of doing all the dirty work."

"Thorn! Stop being crass." I couldn't resist laughing.

Just imagining Thorn Grantham servicing himself brought heat to my cheeks. "We have sex all the time."

"Am I asleep when it happens?"

With a gentle shove, I pushed him out of the bed. "All we'll do is sleep tonight if you don't take a shower so we can go shopping."

As he got into the shower though, I couldn't resist frowning. This was what we always did when I dodged his advances during the full moon. I couldn't keep doing this to him. To us. I shuffled my feet, looking for reasons to feel like I was ready. But how the hell did someone who swam in doubts everyday come to terms with how they'd be as a parent?

I loved Thorn with all my being and did what I thought was impossible to save him nearly a year ago, but sometimes things seemed still insurmountable to me.

The cool rain pelting my face didn't stop me from my shopping trip. Jersey winters laughed at what the Southerners called a winter chill. I'd traipsed through snow drifts for a sale and a bunch of wind wasn't gonna keep me from perusing antique shops and getting my rocks off feeling up old antebellum-era tables and delicate afternoon tea sets.

The antique shops we visited blended into one and the next one, but the prevailing thing was the smells. The richness of the old wood. The faint touch of vanilla and lavender on a cotton and lace bonnet. As I browsed the aisles, I ran my fingers against bureaus from the early 1800s to ribbon-wrapped jars of jams with fresh strawberries inside. Every clerk had a smile for us, asking if we were newlyweds on our honeymoon.

The most interesting shop though was a tiny business right next to a crumbling Piggly Wiggly, the only grocery store in Bright Haven. A covered porch extended from the front, protecting an elderly gentleman who tipped back and forth in a creaky rocking chair. As grocery store shoppers passed, they'd nod to him, but he kept on going, not paying them any mind. His rocker was just far enough from the line of rain to keep him dry.

As we passed him to the tiny shop, he murmured, "You should be careful digging up holes when you don't know what you'll find."

His paper-thin voice was so whispery it barely registered over the pitter-patter of the rain on the tin roof.

"Excuse me?" I asked.

The old man didn't respond, merely continuing the steady motion of his rocking. I shrugged and went inside. The storefront for Lilly Mae's Antique Emporium was only a narrow bay window with a headless, barely-clothed mannequin, but on the inside, the shop extended far into the back. A few select lights here and there illuminated the space. Curiosity tugged me inside. The air here was far stuffier than most places. Almost as if every morning the doors were shut for years and only re-opened for inquisitive souls like me.

The sounds of shuffling from the back reached my ears. A shadow grew along the wall until I spied an older woman wearing an ill-fitted, dark brown dress waddling our way. "Can I help you?" A fog of jasmine enveloped me. The werewolf had dabbed herself a few too many times.

I smiled at her. "Not yet. I'm visiting from out of town to see if anything catches my eye."

She nodded, adjusting the black wig on her head. Bits of her white hair peeked from underneath. Instead of leaving us to browse, she hovered close as if we'd need help right then and there. Not far from me, I spotted a strange, black box with shiny tools inside. One of them appeared to be a long, metal pick. The other one was a hammer. A shudder ran through me when I read the words *Transorbital Lobotomy Kit* in cursive on a tiny card next to the box.

Thorn cocked a grin as he found a spot to hold up the wall. He'd probably read the news on his smartphone until I was done shopping. At least he wasn't the one with a tagalong.

"Is your friend from around here?" she whispered. Discretion was a southerner's best friend. The other best friend was gossip.

"No, my husband isn't," I said.

"Your husband? He's handsome." She paused for a moment as if in deep thought. "I have a granddaughter I should introduce him to."

Thorn chuckled when he heard her.

"How *sweet?*" What else could I say? *Look, Granny, he's married. As in taken. So send your granddaughter's honey and biscuits to some other hungry wolf.*

The elderly werewolf continued to follow me as I looked over some jewelry cases. It was rather hard to enjoy the craftsmanship though.

"He looks so familiar," the woman said from close behind me. "Does he have kin around here?"

"Not that I know of."

"I wish I could remember where I saw a face similar to his. Anyway," her voice strangely brightened, "you two should be careful since there's a rumor around about a town curse."

My hand froze on the edge of the container I was holding. "Excuse me?"

Thorn's head slowly lifted.

"I refuse to live in town. I come here every day to operate my shop, and I've always wondered." Her gaze floated away for a moment before she met my eyes again. "Haven't you taken a look around this place? The buildings? The way a darkness settled around the corners of every home?"

The need to humor her was obvious. A moment before, she wanted to introduce a married man to her granddaughter—if she had one—but she had a point. And that was what concerned me the most.

"The town is rundown, but that doesn't mean it's cursed." Magic was something I didn't trifle with—in any form, but the rumblings of a touched werewolf shouldn't have kept Thorn and I from enjoying our weekend.

"Now I remember." She moved in close enough to violate my personal space, so I took a polite step back. "Is your friend's last name Grantham?"

"Yes, it is," Thorn joined us.

From our past conversations, all I knew was that the Granthams emigrated from Europe to the United States long before my family came. I listened for many hours to my grandma Lasovskaya talk about her journey from Russia to the US, but Thorn never revealed his family history.

She chuckled, briefly reaching out with her thin fingers to touch him. "I've seen a face like yours on a photo from an album. Those men were Union soldiers, a bunch of handsome boys in blue. The one who looked like you had the name Oswald Grantham."

After hearing that name, Thorn perked up. "Where can we find this album? Do you have it?"

"Oh, no." She shook her head. "The pack alpha bought

most of my Civil War memorabilia a few years ago. He's kind of batshit crazy."

Thorn and I exchanged a look. Now that was definitely the pot calling the kettle black.

"If you ask him, he might dig into his collection and let you know more about the man in the picture," the shopkeeper said. "Most of what we have in town is connected to the area."

Thorn nodded, and we thanked her for her time.

As much as I wanted to hear more, the shadows here seemed too stifling to linger.

Sunset approached far faster than I'd expected. After a quick dinner at a local diner, we returned to the bed and breakfast to get ready for the ceremony. As hints of the moon rising touched me, my skin hummed from the oncoming change. In a few hours, I would be hunting beside Thorn as a wolf. The monthly ritual was our time alone in our natural forms.

Thorn dressed in a white shirt and black formal slacks while I put on a long, white gown made from the softest chiffon and silk. I didn't have anything nice back at home, so my aunt Olga was kind enough to loan me one of her Russian pageant dresses from back in the day—the late eighties, to be honest—but her kindness was appreciated, so I accepted the dress with grace.

"It's classic, Nat," she said with a swirl of her fingers. "This dress never goes out of style."

Thorn didn't complain. The garment clung to every curve I had, and based on the hungry look he gave me, I did the dress justice.

"So ..." Thorn drew my body against the hard lines of

his. Damn, he smelled so good. "Do we start the mating ritual before the ceremony or after?" His lips trailed along my jaw line, sending delicious sparks in their wake.

Before I replied, I had to swallow past the lump in my throat. "They want us down in the fortress before sunset."

He drew me into a kiss as his large hands rubbed the bared skin of my back. Warmth spread from each stroke. Our kiss deepened, and I couldn't resist moaning. He tasted amazing. All I could do was clench his wide back and hold on for the ride.

"We can start early on the baby-making if you like. I wouldn't mind getting you out of these clothes twice." The low timbre of his voice melted my insides, but the reality of the situation also pressed against my mind. I was Fertile Myrtle tonight—whether I was ready or not.

I froze.

"You know how I feel," I whispered.

He continued to hold me close, but I sensed a wall crash down between us as he sighed.

"And how *do* you feel?" he managed, probably trying not to sound too upset.

He tried to kiss me again, but I added some space between us. As much as I wanted to dance the horizontal mambo with Thorn, I wasn't ready for pregnancy. I had too many reasons that I didn't feel like rehashing with him.

Also, I was a stickler for time. The clock read five-thirty. We didn't have time to make out like two horny college kids.

He took my hand. I sensed his blue eyes on me, but I didn't want to look at them. To remember all the beautiful things he told me the last time we had this discussion:

I choose you as my consort.

You're perfect in all the right places. Our baby would be the same.

Your mental illness hasn't kept you from overcoming the challenges in your life.

I had faced many challenges, including dealing with an obsessive-compulsive disorder, but bringing a kid into this world was a game-changer. A life-altering event that even my willpower couldn't swallow whole. Just hearing Thorn say those things wasn't the same as believing *without* a doubt. Something I wasn't sure I could do.

Instead of tugging him into my arms to surrender to desire, I pulled him toward the door. It was time for the ceremony. Dealing with the next major step in our lives was best suited for after the wedding vows and the light of the morning.

A wide, dirt path took us from the sidewalk toward the Bright Haven Fortress ruins. The sun peeked from the horizon, and a purple haze bled through the trees, giving them an ominous glow. Thorn continued to hold my hand as we walked toward the columns without words.

Maybe he was mad at me. When I squeezed his hand, he didn't squeeze back. That was a first for Thorn. He was rarely perturbed by what I threw at him, but I guessed everyone had limits.

As much as I wanted to see his side of things, it was hard. Living as a werewolf wasn't an easy existence. A rival pack attacked ours over a year ago. There were enemies within our ranks that searched for any opportunity to bring down Thorn and me. How could I possibly protect a baby in that situation?

He did look at me, but he must've sensed my thoughts. "You have the largest family I've ever seen." He chuckled.

"You'd never be alone. You're never alone when you have your pack and the people you love around you."

The trees obscuring the ruins came into the view, and with it, the lights from torches inside the hollowed out building. To my left, I spied in the growing darkness headstones. Most likely from soldiers who never survived countless attacks. The dates stood out in the carved, moss-covered limestone. 1878. 1733. To think Thorn and I would live for centuries if we took care of each other was mind boggling at times.

The sounds of voices bounced around the open space inside the ruins. A sizeable crowd gathered with a few recognizable faces from our shopping trip. The older werewolf from the Lilly Mae's Antique Emporium waved at me. And she wasn't alone either. She pointed to a young woman, who was most likely her single granddaughter, and winked at Thorn. A few women huddled around a long table, setting up a wedding cake and appetizers. One man continued to light torches in the circle they formed around us.

"It's almost sunset," Jackson said with enthusiasm. He came up behind us and pushed us toward a single stone block near the front of the fortress. "We should get you two taken care of ... before the sun goes down."

"Sorry," I murmured. "We needed to talk for a bit."

"Not a problem. How about we get started?" He glanced to the pack alpha and his wife who waited for us. "Our alpha wanted to say a few words before your ceremony began. He'll be sure to be *brief*."

I tried not to laugh. The last thing we needed was for everyone to shift into werewolves and have a bunch of dogs ransacking the food table. The twinges of the change should've hit me hard about now, but I felt fine. Maybe I had enough control to last through the ceremony. Thorn could always control his shape-shifting until the last minute.

Calvin stepped forward. "These are the Bright Haven Fort ruins. As both a boy and as a man, I've seen the honorable structure in its glory days and now I see her in her wreckage. Precious moments like your vows tonight remind us that once what was tainted can become clean again. Through the ceremonies we hold here, we can only hope you two see past any differences you have and agree that a united front is better than a divided one."

I sensed Thorn's deep blue eyes on me, but I couldn't hold his gaze. So far, I hadn't done too well on the united front part.

Beyond Thorn's back, I spotted what was left of the sun as it sank toward the horizon. It glowed against his back, creating an angelic hue. I snorted and tried not to think about the devilish things he planned for me tonight.

"You're not a part of our pack," Calvin said as he continued, "but the bonds between you and your mate can be declared anywhere with a dominant pair present. Please speak your minds."

Thorn faced me, and I swallowed the well of feelings that sprang. A smile spread across his face, and for a moment, it was just us. His hands in mine. The breeze ruffling his hair. The deep scent of old stone and thick Spanish moss.

Not far from me, I caught the nervous gaze of the mayor. His eyes kept flicking to the alpha pair. *What had him so twitchy?* A disturbing sense of unease crept up the back of spine.

"The first time we did this, you were tired, I was tired." Thorn had my attention again, and I was lulled in to his words, remembering. "You'd fought for your life that night to become my alpha female. Now matter what would've happened, you would have always had my heart. I choose you for all the things that make you perfect for me." He reached out a hand and wiped something off my cheek. I hadn't realized I'd started crying.

"Now that we're making strides in our relationship, I wanted to give you the moment you deserved—"

Suddenly, a shriek filled the ruins. Followed by another. Thorn's grip on my hands tightened and he pushed me behind him toward the center of the fort.

"What was that?" I said.

"It sounded human," Thorn replied.

Beyond the ruins, someone raced across the field in the murky darkness. Then two more people ran to our right. The sounds of their footsteps and rapid heartbeats filled my senses. Beyond them, I noticed the sun had set. Darkness prevailed and leached toward the columns beyond the fortress.

Instead of backing toward us in a defensive formation like any group of werewolves would, the wedding party members glumly stood there looking at us.

Had the drinking started too soon and I missed something?

"We'd hoped you'd finish the ceremony first before things got complicated," Jackson said slowly.

"Complicated?" Thorn said, the growing tension thinning his voice.

Uncontrollable laughter, followed by the sounds of shattered glass came from farther away.

The mayor sighed. "Many years ago, someone cursed our town and the people who live here."

Dread kicked me in the gut. So what the shopper keeper said was true? Had something happened to all the humans?

He took a step away from us and appeared to be crest-fallen. "Things around here have gotten pretty bad."

"No shit," I whispered.

"We need to leave," Thorn said firmly.

"Please don't go," the alpha female said. Calvin continued to stand silent like the stone walls around us. "We've invited so many couples. They came—and ate our food—but none of them succeeded in removing the curse."

"Maybe because you brought them here under false pretenses," I spat. The desire to leave grew, but something told me to stay put and learn the real deal. "Give it to me straight."

Thorn trembled at my side, his anger building.

"Look, look. Here is where things stand—" the mayor began.

"Stop feeding them bullshit, Jackson," Calvin said. He looked me square in the eyes, and I did the same to him.

"Not long after the Yankees took out this fortress during the Civil War, one of our ancestors tainted this town with a curse," Calvin began. "Ever since then, no werewolf living in town shifts into their natural form during the full moon. Overnight, all the pack members fall into madness, but by dawn, everything resets back to how it was before." He let out a long sigh. "The town has deteriorated since that time."

The mayor held his head down, avoiding our hard stare. "The Granthams won't help us like the others. They'll run away."

"They will help," the alpha implored. "They have no choice."

No choice in what?

My gaze snapped to Thorn's. Icy fear slithered up my back and wrapped around my throat like a tightening vice.

I took a step away from them, and then I sensed it—or

perhaps the better term was what I *didn't* sense. Between the cries from the crowd around us, the town beyond the fortress had gone silent. The song from the wind whistling between the columns muted. My heartbeat's rapid pitter-patter faded away, too.

Even worse, the moon's siren call for me to shift into wolf form never reached my ears. The itch to shift was gone. With growing horror building into a heavy iron block in my stomach, I stared at my husband.

"We're cursed, too," he gasped.

CHAPTER 4

Everyone faced each other, no one moving until a man shrieked like a night owl as he streaked butt-naked across the field. Another woman, not a single stitch of clothing either, made a beeline for the refreshments table and tackled everyone around it before she landed onto it. On top of our cake, too. With a gleeful expression on her face, she shoved handfuls of cake into her mouth. Then she flung a fistful of cake at the mayor. With a wet plop, a healthy dollop of icing struck the side of his face.

Two dark-haired, half-naked men advanced on us from right. One diverted his path to pounce on the alpha. Calvin rolled out of his attack, tossing the pouncing man into the fortress wall. Thorn and I stood watching the madness like fools until he grabbed my hand and as we made a run for it, I ditched the heels and ran barefoot out of the ruins.

"Where are we going?" I already sounded breathless as we reached the street. My lungs burned as he led me around a corner, but we kept running. All the lights from the houses were out. There was no one on the streets—except those who chased after us.

The need to look behind me tugged at me. For so long I'd depended on my ears to hear pursuers but they sounded so far away. When I glanced over my shoulder, I was stunned and gripped Thorn's arm.

"They're closing in on us," I yelled.

Thorn noticed broken glass on the sidewalk so he hoisted me over his shoulder and kept going into the street.

"This isn't a smart move," I belted out.

He put me back down once we reached a dark alley. "This is so gross," I hissed into his ear. We hid behind a garbage container. I ignored the rising disgust, but it threatened to overtake me. All the things I could ignore before came full force in an inhale and exhale—from the sidewalk to the alley to the filthy waste receptacle beside us. This wasn't the time for my obsessive-compulsive disorder to kick in full strength.

I closed my eyes and took a deep breath. In through the nose and out through the mouth. *I'm okay. I'm okay. I'm okay.*

"Why aren't they coming after us?" I whispered, trying to think of anything except our predicament. My anxiety skyrocketed since our human form locked us. The wolf in me, the part that didn't care about the trivial things humans cared about, was silent.

"They can't hear or smell us," he replied.

We exchanged a look. "Those crazy bastards are as human as we are."

He nodded and rubbed his arms.

I noticed the cold then, too. Normally our warm bodies never noticed temperatures a few degrees above freezing, but right then, I couldn't help but feel the icy breeze that swept down the alley and went up my dress. Wow, that kind of cold was something the humans felt all the time. What a bummer.

"We need to get our clothes and coats." A look of determination crossed his face. "You stay here where it's safe and dark. I'll hurry back to the B&B to get our stuff. Once I get back, we'll get the hell out of this place."

I grabbed his arm. "I'm not saying here by myself."

He sighed. "Things are difference now. You're different —" He stopped then added, "We're both different. The sooner we get to safety the better—"

I couldn't stop my bitter retort from coming fast. "You mean I'm even weaker now."

"I didn't say that, Natalya."

"But did you think it?"

He held my face between his large hands. "I didn't think it. If you really used that smart head of yours, you'd know I'm the weaker one right now. I may look like I've got my shit together, but right now I'm pretty messed up inside."

I had calmed myself through controlled breathing. Attending group therapy for my anxiety taught me a trick or two on coping with stress.

"You're not going alone," I said. "We need to stay together."

He finally nodded, relenting to my stern expression.

He took my hand and led me out of the alley back into the street. We took things slowly, aiming for stealth like any good hunter would do. We darted from building to building, car to car, until we reached the outside of the Uncle Barker's Bed and Breakfast. The flashy Christmas lights were turned off, and now the beautiful building had a dark presence. Thorn and I considered going through the front door, but we noticed two half-naked folks lounging around the sign. They picked at the Christmas lights while the other one plucked the heads off the wilted orchids in the flowerbed. It was a damn shame they had to deface one the prettiest parts of the property.

The only option left was to try the back of the building or to climb up the side somehow. Each floor had a balcony. With some hard work, we could get to our second-floor room. We headed for the side and approached one of the trellises reaching to the second floor.

"Will it hold your weight?" I asked him.

He checked and nodded.

Before he went though, he gestured for me to head on up first. Under normal circumstances, a quick leap to a second floor could be done without an afterthought. Now we were dropped down a peg or two in terms of strength. I grabbed the side of the trellis and barely got a few feet. It was embarrassing to say the least.

"Give me a boost," I hissed.

"How?" He grabbed me around the waist and heaved me up as far as he could. "I hadn't realized you were this heavy," he said with a chuckle.

"You are so dead when this is over, Grantham."

Somehow, we managed to climb the trellis and enter our room through the unlocked balcony door. The house was silent. Far too silent for what I preferred. Usually the furnace or the fridge faintly hummed. This never ending silence where all I heard was my own breathing and the rustle of clothing as I took off my dress to put on some jeans and Thorn put on his coat was disturbing.

All I had left was a rising sense of dread. Some of these townspeople seemed harmless, but the ones who had chased us and even the man who viciously attacked the pack alpha, they lost all sense and now ransacked the town into the state it was in now. They'd destroyed it themselves.

Thorn clutched the keys in his hands. "We need to go."

"Wait a minute."

"What's wrong?" he asked.

I wrung my hands together. "What if this is permanent?"

"He said the townspeople are like this. The minute we leave this place, we should go back to normal."

"But he said something specific. *The people who lived here.* Living some place could imply staying for a period of time. It's a vague statement, yes, but what if we go back home and we end up like these people?"

He searched my face as if an answer would come, but it didn't. He gathered me into his arms, and I sensed his fierce need to protect me fighting with his desire to do the right thing. A pack leader always protected their own. Even to the death. Running away was a potential solution, but it might not be the right one.

Families still lived here. Men, women, and children who depended on visitors—or should I say victims—to help them out of the bind they'd gotten into. One thing I'd learned from my family was to do the honorable thing.

One look at my face and he sighed.

"So what now, wife?" he asked.

"CALVIN SAID at dawn everything resets—that everyone goes back to normal." I rubbed my face with my hands, hoping I'd keep my wits about me long enough to figure out a solution. "So we need to find the cause of the curse—whatever it is."

Thorn nodded. "While we look for the cause, we'll have to be content with being surrounded by a bunch of crazies?"

"Pretty much. Now let's see if I can figure things out." I paced the room, trying to be quiet as possible but allowing myself to think. "Didn't the shopkeeper *and* the alpha say that the town's problems began when the fort was rebuilt a second time after the Civil War? And that the decline slowly occurred *after* the pack alpha returned home from war?"

"That sounds about right. Do you think Cal could be behind all this?"

"I think so. What events—that we know about—could cause a curse? Most curses come from injustice. An event occurs where a wrong is committed ..."

Everything came together, almost like an audible click in my noggin.

"It has to be that crazy bastard," I said. "Remember the story with the woman and the strange figurine?"

Thorn nodded.

"What if she was a witch? And she cursed him for taking her figurine?" I asked.

"That sounds possible, but how do we find it?"

"Oh, that's easy. Guess who is the town heirloom collector, or should I say fellow antique junkie like me?" I added.

Thorn scoffed. "I wouldn't put the two of you in any group together."

"You have a point there."

A sound from down the hallway made Thorn freeze. He glanced at me, pointed to the doorway, and then pointed to his ears. I expected him to use body language, as a wolf everything was subtle, a glance of the eyes, the way his body would shift toward a place where he caught a sound. Thorn might've been human now, but a part of the wolf still swam underneath his skin. Without a sound, he moved to the door and pressed his ear against the old wood to listen.

He whispered something, but I didn't catch it. A few seconds later, he waved at me toward the window.

This lack of enhanced hearing took some getting used to.

From the balcony, Thorn climbed down the trellis first. He dropped our bags into a heavy fog that slithered across the ground.

I flashed him a look as to why he grabbed our bags and his smirk practically screamed, "Do you wanna stay here after we save the day?"

He had a point there.

As I followed him, I immediately wondered how I'd get

down. Leaping to the fog below wasn't the smartest idea. Not when it was so thick I swore it might swallow me into the swampy earth below. I angled myself off the balcony's edge, using a death-grip on the railing until I found solid footing to climb down the trellis. Thorn waited with his arms stretched wide.

We found a quiet corner while I looked up the alpha's address.

"Do you expect to find him in the local yellow pages?" Thorn asked.

"I seriously doubt the alpha, who was alive during the Civil War period, will live in one of these tiny run down places. If I was him—and I believe he thinks like me—he will live in the oldest house around here with enough space to satisfy a hoarder." As I scanned the cellphone screen, I found what I was looking for and presented my findings with a smug expression.

He just shook his head.

I could get used to this being right thing.

Calvin's place was on the outskirts of Bright Haven, to the north of town. We'd passed the long driveway to his home and hadn't even known it. Cypresses covered with thick Spanish moss obscured the driveway, the limbs extended toward the narrow road. The dirt path was riddled with puddles and plenty of potholes. Thorn drove the SUV up toward the house. As we closed in, he turned off the lights.

"What are you doing?" I tried to peer through the fog into the darkness, but I couldn't see much.

"Do you want whoever lives here to see us?" he replied.

"What good will sneaking up on him do if we run into a tree?"

Thorn slowed to a crawl for the rest of the way until we

spotted an expansive two-story home. There weren't any other cars in the driveway. Maybe Calvin and his wife were trying to clean up the mess in town to keep other pack members safe.

Stone columns, lined with moss peeking out of the cracks were at the edges of a stone walkway toward the house. The wide porch hadn't seen repair in a while from what I could see. As we got out of the SUV and quietly made our way toward the house, the only thing we spotted was the movement from a large owl diving from one of the trees toward the house. It perched on the rooftop and peered at us as if we were prey.

I tried to listen, to feel for whatever could be coming for us, but it was damn near impossible. How did humans live from day to day without getting taken out as a species?

Thorn took a step on the porch, and the wood groaned. He hesitated then tried another path that didn't look as old. That was rather hard. The porch hadn't seen a fresh coat of paint in years. The chairs, which appeared so welcoming from a distance, had cobwebs clinging to their corners. A pitcher, filled with gunky water, sat on the ledge.

Lemonade, anyone?

We didn't expect to see inside, but the ornate oak doorway was wide open and swayed with the breeze, almost inviting us in. I slowed down, but Thorn took my hand and led the way inside. Beyond the porch, we entered what could be called a mudroom. The floor sighed and creaked with each step. If we expected to make a quiet entrance that opportunity was blown. My gaze took in the expansive foyer, the chandelier lit from the moonlight bleeding though the doorway. When the shopkeeper said Calvin loved to collect memorabilia, she wasn't kidding. Along the wallpapered walls in the foyer, I spotted shelf after shelf after shelf with guns, sharp weapons in cases, vases, and other dusty antiques.

But no statute that looked like a wooden relic so far.

From the foyer, an elaborate staircase extended to the second floor, to a sitting room to our right, and toward a dark hallway. I glanced into the sitting room and gasped. From one end to the other of the sitting room was nothing but animal heads on the walls. Elk, bucks, an elephant, too. Yet it was the five heads displayed in the center that made my skin crawl the wrong way. The mounted heads of five wolves stared at us with glassy eyes. With each step I took, I felt like their gaze followed me.

According the laws that governed werewolves, hunting regular wolves was a forbidden act. They were intelligent kin to be respected unless they openly attacked. To hunt them was like hunting your own kind.

Not far from me, Thorn clenched his fists.

"Let's go," he whispered. "We've got a job to do."

After checking out the room, we decided to head up the stairs to see if we could find where Cal stored his personal belongings. The padded staircase remained hushed and we plodded up them to the second floor. This whole house had such strong bones. It was a shame that dust covered the paintings of beautiful women in 19th century attire. From the top of the stairs, we had a few options, but Thorn suggested we try the double doors. Thorn took point, opening the brass knob. He checked inside then beckoned me with a flick of his fingers. Calvin's master bedroom, unlike the rest of his house, was maintained to perfection. Candles pushed away the room's shadows. The poster bed was beautiful, taking up the far right side of the room, while his sitting area to the left had a full seating to accommodate a quiet evening for the couple. As to why the television tray with crackers and cheese messed up the scene, I didn't speculate.

As I took a step farther inside, I spied our prize on a white pedestal along the opposite wall: a dark wooden statue, over a foot in height, heavy at the bottom and curving upward into the form of a ripe pear. A plump bosom down to wide hips. An African fertility goddess. As I took in the relic, I could almost see Calvin standing above that poor slave, the butt of his rifle raised to slam it into her face. He was dressed in his gray Confederate uniform and wore the smug expression he had during dinner. A man like him—one who took what didn't belong to him and harmed the defenseless—didn't deserve such a prize.

Suddenly, a hand circled my throat from behind and pressed a knife to my pulse point.

"You're a smarter gal than I thought you'd be," a low voice drawled in my ear. "Keep quiet, bitch."

Thorn kept walking. He hadn't heard a damn thing.

As Cal tried to pull me backward, I shuffled my feet as loudly as I could.

Thorn whipped around and advanced on us.

"Ah, ah, ah ..." Calvin flashed the knife, and it glinted against the glow from the candles. "Stay back unless you want a demonstration of how slowly she'll heal now."

Thorn froze, a menacing growl building in his throat.

Cal laughed. "It's been a long time since I've been able to do that."

Thorn's blue eyes darkened. "If you hurt her ..."

"If I hurt her, you'll do what? When I learned about your name, I wondered if you were as cowardly as another Grantham I met many, many years ago. What was his name again?"

"Oswald Grantham?" I supplied.

Thorn flashed me an exasperated look.

"Yep, that was the boy's name," Calvin said. "A newborn pup had more spunk than Oswald. A flea could knock a man's ass over faster 'n his fist."

Thorn's jawline twitched, but nothing else moved. The light was dim in here, but I could've sworn he hunched over a little, almost as if he wanted to shift. Had he succeeded?

"I'm quite impressed. Only one other alpha made it to my house. His grandfather had fought with me at Fort Sumter. A brave man he was, but when you stripped away the wolf, all that was left was a husk of a man." Calvin pushed me hard to the floor. "Are you weak?"

"Why don't you come and find out?" Thorn growled.

My knees hit the floor hard, the pain reverberating up my leg. As much I wanted to sit there and recover, this asshole rubbed my fur the wrong way.

"He's not weak, and neither am I." I stood and threw a right hook across his chin. The moment my fist connected with his jawbone, I knew my mistake.

Crunch!

"Son-of-a-bitch!" I shouted.

Now that was new. Pain from throwing a punch.

I clutched my hand and took a step back as Cal laughed. He rubbed his chin. "Not bad."

"How about this?" Thorn swept forward, ramming into Calvin. He rained punches into Calvin's right side. I expected to see the alpha's face contort in pain, but he sneered and sidestepped behind Thorn. With smooth movements, he slammed his fist onto the middle of Thorn's back.

"No!" I rushed at them as Thorn groaned and fell to his knees, clenching his lower spine. Before Calvin could land another punch, I careened at that crazy bastard, swinging again—broken hand be damned. I bared my tiny human teeth at him, tackling into his side. My puny punches didn't do much damage, and that showed as Calvin flung me to the floor again. My head hit the hardwood with a thud, the world around me shifting like riding upside down on a swinging tire.

Calvin took a defensive stance as Thorn came in hard with a right hook followed by a left that made contact with Calvin's face. Blood ran down the alpha's split lip and already the signs of bruising marred his face.

Using his right shoulder, Thorn rammed Calvin into the far wall and they knocked over the pedestal. The relic crashed to the floor and rolled toward the fireplace near the seating area. I crawled after it as the sounds of flesh punching flesh came from behind me. The two men stumbled toward me, Thorn in a headlock as they rolled to the floor.

"Thorn, what are you doing?" I called.

"Getting choked to death!" he spouted.

Thorn roared and managed to raise Calvin on his back. My husband's face blossomed red from the lack of air, but with a final push, he backed hard into one of the solid wood bedposts. Meanwhile, I scrambled to the relic and managed to get a good grip on it.

I tried to stand on steady feet, but the world wobbled a bit. I swallowed back the nausea and advanced on them. Thorn's eyes rolled up the back of his head. Calvin refused to let go.

"Defend against this!" I raised the statue high above my head, and walloped Calvin across the head. He staggered a bit, so I hit him one more time. With a heavy thud, my husband landed hard on the floor with Calvin collapsed on top of him.

I released a long sigh. "I hate dogpiles."

Getting Calvin's dead weight off my husband was difficult, but I managed to free Thorn. He was breathless and a bit dizzy too, but he'd survived.

I touched his poor face. On any other day he was perfection, chiseled cheeks, the kind of face stubble a woman wanted to touch. Right then, he was a hot mess of blood, bruises, and cuts.

The man I'd fallen in love with.

"How bad is it?" He stumbled over a few words since his lip swelled up.

"You look perfect. We should take a couple selfie." I fished for my camera, but he backed away.

His laugh was throaty as we staggered out of the room.

"So what do we do with it?" he asked me.

Now that was a fifty million dollar question. My head refused to think straight from the hit to my head. "What did that woman want to do with it? Before he took it from her?"

He glanced toward the ceiling as if searching his memories. "She wanted to bury it."

"Let's try that," I said with a groan. What I wouldn't give for some headache meds.

"Are you sure?"

"Can you think of anything else?"

He sighed. "How far should we go to bury it?"

"The way I'm feeling right now, if there was a flowerpot with dirt, I'd be game."

"Backyard, it is."

We got down the stairs—without falling down them—and we managed to reach the expansive front yard.

"If we hide it here, won't he find it in the morning?" I asked Thorn.

"How about the backyard in the woods?"

Once we found a good spot, we got to work. Side by side, we used our hands to dig a hole in the rich mud in the backyard. I should've folded over from the worms, filth, and dirt, but right then, I was too weak and tired to care. I was alive with my husband at my side and there we were, like a bunch of fools digging into the Georgia clay to bury the statue. As I placed it into the two-foot hole we'd dug, the heavy wood warmed my hands. I ran my fingers along the marble-smooth curves, wondering what powers the statue held. Was the woman truly some kind of spellcaster, maybe a witch? After encountering amazing people and seeing the impossible become possible, just holding this figurine and making what was wrong right again made me feel like for this one moment in time I could withstand anything.

Like my future with Thorn.

"Whatever grievances you have," I whispered, "I hope this will make amends." And, I added, "We beat his ass pretty badly."

Thorn left my side as I began to cover the hole. "What are you doing?" I asked him.

"I need to make sure he doesn't find it. We need to leave our scent all over the place." Thorn dug up and reburied countless holes as I hid the figurine under the dirt and brush. As the reddish-purple sun rose on the horizon, a world of scents opened up to me. The wind brought a bouquet of seedling wildflowers. A chorus of birds and insects greeted me.

We had lifted the curse.

I shrugged off my coat as the heat from working got diffi-cult. Not far from me, I caught my husband's scent. Every now and then, he glanced at me, even winking at me once. The night of the full moon was now over, but we'd survived the night together. Even at our weakest.

By the time we left in the SUV, Thorn's face looked a lot better compared to a few hours before. I'd snapped a quick picture when he was at his worst. Once we were on the road, he voiced his concern.

"What's the purpose of taking my picture while I was digging?" he asked.

"When are we ever going to have a memory of you looking like that? You're always so *perfect*. And anyway, a photo like that is album material. Wedding album material."

"Don't be surprised if you find it missing. I could never live that up with the pack."

"So you'd tell our future children their dad was too much of a punk to stand showing his weak side? Even for one night?"

At my words, his face softened. "Future children?"

I took his hand, and our fingers intertwined. "After tonight, I think I'd be open to talking about it more."

"Why the change of heart?"

"I don't know, really. I think it was when I saw Calvin holding you like that. As a human, you are so vulnerable. So much more than all the times you risked life and limb for me. I don't want to let go of you or what we have. Even at our weakest we pulled through." Raw emotion welled up inside me, but I tried to push it away and failed. "Together. We did it together."

"Those are the best vows I've ever heard, sweetheart."

He drew my hand to his lips and kissed it. I laughed.

"What's so funny?" he asked.

"A few hours ago, that kiss would've hurt like hell."

"So you're saying the human thing isn't for you?"

"Give me butt-naked transformation, howling at the moon, and obnoxious pack behavior all day. This living as a human thing is not for us."

Suddenly, he pulled over to the side of the deserted road. He turned toward me after he killed the engine. "And what about mating?"

"The full moon is over, you know."

"I don't need the need the full moon to want to make love to my wife." He closed in on me, leaning over the seat. The scent of his desire filled my nostrils and caressed my body.

"Aren't you tired from all that fighting?" My voice was already breathless.

"When we get back to Jersey, we can sleep all we want. For now, I got some catching up to do."

He kissed me, enveloping me in his arms, and I knew I wouldn't have it any other way.

The End

AN AMUSING WEEKEND

CHAPTER 1

Reader Note: This story takes place after Compelled (Coveted #3)

I'M ABOUT to have the best weekend ever.

If I survive group therapy for my anxiety, that is.

The coffee cup in my hand had already gone cold, but the session had yet to begin. I re-crossed my legs.

"You look like you're at the starting line for the Olympics, Natalya," the brunette next to me said softly. "In forty-five minutes this will all be over..."

She did have a point there. For the last ten minutes, my heeled foot tapped against the floor. An annoyed *twap, twap, twap* noise. But the thing is, as much as I try to control my anxiety, especially during group therapy, reining it in is difficult. You see, for over a year, I've been attending while under the watchful eye of a white wizard named Dr. Frank. So far he'd been able to see past any of the tricks I tried to pull. My *little* shopping habit being one of them.

But Dr. Frank isn't here today.

Matter of fact, six people sat in a circle with one empty

chair and Dr. Frank was nowhere to be seen. So we had no choice but to look at each other and wait. The brunette next to me, Abby the muse, was quite patient. Matter of fact, she had enough patience for both of us. She sat with her legs crossed, her hands placed perfectly in her lap, and not once did she bother to eat the week-old, fruit-filled doughnuts or attempt to sample the coffee I couldn't classify as such. (Another group therapy attendee hadn't restrained herself.) Naturally, I picked up my own caffeine fuel on the way into Manhattan from Jersey.

Dr. Frank usually walked in with a smile, but our replacement dematerialized into the empty chair. Poor Abby jumped like she was about to get mugged.

The blonde woman glanced at each of us, her face reflecting exasperation. I should be the one who's exasperated. I could've been doing so many other things—like shopping for unnecessary trinkets in Times Square.

Werewolves are the worst people to attend therapy. Most of the time, the wolf inside of me is like an animal circling inside of a cage. One would think it would be lying there gnawing on a doggie toy, but today, just a few days before the full moon, my insides churned and a never-ending hunger urged me to hunt. As much as I wanted to chase down cottontails in sunny meadows, I had to be responsible and see what this lady had to say.

The therapist finally spoke. "Dr. Frank still isn't available, but the good news is I'm here!"

Hurray?

She continued. "I am Dr. Greta Peabottom, and I'm filling in for your therapist for the foreseeable future."

Dr. Peabottom...what a wonderful name. Too bad she's a witch. Not that I discriminate or anything. But, here's the thing: most spellcasters, if they are witches or warlocks aren't healers. Wizards are the only ones who can do white magic well while warlocks dabble in dark and light magic. I've seen warlocks try to heal and I've done a better job with bleeders using gauze and duck tape.

Which left me with an obvious question: How the hell was she going to heal anybody? Before all sessions started Dr. Frank relieved our anxiety with a spell or two that had the equivalent jolt of Vicodin covered in rainbows.

"Let's begin with deep motivational breathing," Dr. Peabottom said softly.

Everyone grinned in anticipation of what was to come. Hell, even I was smiling at this point. I closed my eyes and waited for it, sucking a deep breath in and then out.

A minute passed. Then another thirty seconds. Nothing happened. I opened my eyes and everyone was looking at Dr. Peabottom with distaste. We'd been jilted. As expected the happy-go-lucky, practically trippy, high feeling we got from our doctor was now absent from Dr. Peabottom.

Yep, I was really gonna love this session. Next, our new therapist went into a speech about meditating anxiety away and I tried not to mentally clock out. Compared to several months ago, things were quite different. Two of my closest therapy friends were gone. A nymph I didn't know well sat in Heidi's usual seat. I missed that foul-mouthed mermaid dearly. Right next to the nymph was where Nick used to sit. If he were here, he'd be flashing me a look to remind me to stop being so close-minded.

"How has your week gone?" Dr. Peabottom asked.

This was the standard question Dr. Frank asked too.

The nymph jumped in first, quite eager to get a word out. "For the past two months, I've been dating this guy...I love him so much, but he keeps disappearing for weeks on end. I don't want to be clingy or anything, but I keep crying all the time and I can't seem to stop." She sighed. "I think I'm scaring people who visit my park."

Dr. Peabottom nodded. "Have you talked to him about your agoraphobia?"

The nymph rolled her eyes. "Of course not. He thinks I'm some hippie who likes to camp out in Central Park."

"Is he a human?" Abby asked.

"Yes," she said as she took a bite of those awful donuts. "I told him we could live off the land. I'd do anything for him, but he keeps running away."

I missed my tactless friends. At this moment Heidi the mermaid would have told the nymph to suck it up and find a new man. My succubus pal, Lilith, would've told her she's lucky any man gave her attention.

I just sat there and wished this was all over.

When the therapist turned to Abby to ask how her month had gone, the muse mumbled her reply.

"For the past few weeks, I feel like I'm an actor in a movie with the same scenes over and over again," she said.

I leaned forward. Abby usually talked about how anxious she got seeing into her authors' heads, but this time she'd said something different.

"I go through the motions each time. I arrive, I do my job, I see things most people can't stomach, and then I walk away. It's like I'm living in hell and I don't know how to cope."

"Has Dr. Frank talked to you about coping mechanisms?" Dr. Peabottom asked.

"He told me to pretend it wasn't real. I'm supposed to imagine I'm watching a movie..." She shook her head. "It's not like I'm watching some splatter flick though. I can smell the blood. I can see the horrified look on the victims' faces before they die..."

Around the circle, the others looked away or messed with what they had in their hands. Usually, I was forced to do the same. Seeing a muse was a rarity. I'm sure for Dr. Frank, the idea of helping one was even more difficult.

It's human nature to recoil and avoid violence. How the hell do you get someone used to violence when it wasn't in their nature? I was still unsettled with filthiness once in a while so I wasn't the person to offer advice.

Not long after each member discussed what problems they had that week, Dr. Peabottom concluded the session. As much I would've preferred to feel like I'd made progress in terms of my obsessive compulsive disorder I was ready to get out of there.

Soon enough, Abby and I left Dr. Frank's office in Manhattan, and we were on our way to the parking garage where I'd left my vehicle.

The spring sunshine bled through the clouds, and I knew I'd at least enjoy the ride on the way into upstate New York.

"You couldn't have run out of there fast enough," Abby said.

"I don't know who's much more of a quack, the guy who is a shape shifter and transforms into ducks, or Dr. Peabottom."

The drive into upstate New York was quaint and quiet. The nice thing about Abby is that she tended to blend in with her surroundings. Whenever we stopped for gas and a few snacks, no one waved at her or acknowledged her. As much as I tried to avoid others, especially when I thought they were covered with germs, I couldn't imagine a life like Abby's. As she browsed the aisles no one attempted to avoid her and no one looked at her as if she was strange. It was just as if she wasn't there.

The kinds of things that would do to a person's head were quite apparent and the way she seemed to shrink in on herself. Her shoulders were hunched over and the coat she wore was two sizes too big. Her brown shoes had countless scuffs along the sides. During therapy her brown eyes always seem to shine, but right now, as she stared down the road toward our destination, they'd gone dead.

About an hour into our ride I was glad she finally piped up. "I really appreciate the ride."

"It's not a problem. Heidi would want me to take care of you."

With that comment she grew even quieter. Heidi and Abby always seemed like a pair. The loud and boisterous one and her quiet sidekick. Maybe it was the fact that Heidi didn't take shit from anybody else and always spoke up for her. Heidi forced Abby to exist in a world where humans couldn't see her.

I didn't mind taking care of Abby, but I wasn't as bold as Heidi. If I had to be the one to take Abby on her next assignment, I'd do it.

The forest grew far denser as we traveled northeast. Highway 29 loomed far to the north.

Abby hadn't provided me with many details on her assignment during our text message exchanges, but now that I had her alone in the car I wanted to know more. "So is this author pretty famous?"

"Somewhat...She is definitely on the rise, but she is a bit of a recluse. It's been difficult to get her to go outside of her comfort zone, but whenever we get together what she creates is absolutely brilliant!"

I couldn't wait. If she was heading for the big leagues she *might* have a nice country home. Before I'd worked at The Bends, I'd had a job in Manhattan working for a publishing company. Meeting authors was one of the perks I enjoyed.

Now that I had Abby all alone I had so many questions about how her job worked.

"So for your summons do you call ahead and let the author know you're coming?" I asked.

"No, not really." She played with a strand of her hair as if we talked about a simple gig. "I just show up and then we get to work."

"Then how do you know they'll be home? They could be gallivanting off in the Arctic somewhere."

"Whenever I get an order from the gods, they tell me the exact location where the artist will be and what I need to do for them. They never tell me how long it will take or in what condition the artist will be in, but one thing's always for certain: Betsy Lee is always zoned out by the time I get to her. Once I do my thing, she'll knock out her short story in a weekend."

Wow that's pretty cool.

"Betsy Lee who?" The name didn't ring a bell in my brain.

"Oh, stop, Nat." She finally offered me a bright smile. "You're not allowed to stalk my artists."

As we ventured deeper into the woods, we finally passed through a small village called Dryer. South Toms River would give this place a run for its money. The place's major buildings were nothing more than a post office, grocery store and the gas station. In front of the few craftsman houses that lined the main street, kids played from yard to yard, and the traffic along the street was light.

I didn't see any supernaturals lurking about, but that didn't mean they didn't cling to the shadows and come out when humans slept during the night.

A few miles outside of Dryer we reached a long driveway hidden behind a thicket of maple trees. Excitement raced up my back as we approached a modern, single-story French country style-home. Whoever Abby's author was they had the cash to build a new construction home with a three-car garage and cobblestone sidewalks. Maybe Betsy Lee was someone famous like Nora Roberts.

We pulled up to the house. I reached for the handle to open the car door, but Abby stopped me.

"I'm not sure how to put this, but you can't meet her." Abby had a straight face while she told me this.

"Excuse me?" I blurted.

"Well, when Heidi takes me to my assignments she does me a little bit of a favor."

Now this is where I find out my weekend really is going to go to shit.

Abby finished digging my grave with flourish. "During the whole trip, the author can never know you're here."

CHAPTER 2

"You want me to do *what*?" My question came out a bit harsher than I'd expected, but my friend had just asked me to play the big bad *invisible* wolf.

Abby's mouth opened and closed a few times as if she was trying to think of how to explain the situation.

So I threw in a question. "Does Heidi hide behind the bushes or spend the weekend in the bathroom or something?"

Abby shrugged. "Most of the time, she drops me off so fast I don't have a chance to shut the car door."

"What kind of hot mess is that?"

She chuckled. "That's Heidi. We once hitchhiked to one of my assignments in West Virginia. It was kind of fun. To be honest, I wonder where she goes when she leaves me behind."

The house was gorgeous and she wanted me to just hangout? Not happening. "So she *never* hung out with you?"

"She has...twice. Actually, she's pretty stealthy. We figured out a routine and everything."

How the hell had my weekend started out like this? I groaned and thumped my forehead against the steering wheel. After a few deep breaths, I checked my cellphone to find the nearest hotel room. And I'll be damned, the nearest motel was an hour and a half away. Even the vacation rental by owners didn't have a spare room nearby.

We sat in the car for ten minutes before Abby spoke up. "Is something wrong—"

Instead of letting her finish her question, I grunted a curse or two in Russian and got out of the car. I headed for the front door. Abby followed in a rush.

"What are you doing?" she asked quietly.

"If I'm gonna go in stealth mode, we have to get in first. Unless you plan to sneak in through a window."

She smiled. "Oh, I don't have to do that. I just walk in." And she did just that. The muse waltzed on in like she owned the place.

The foyer was empty. The house wasn't empty though. I faintly caught sounds of movement.

"We're in the country and all, but who in their right mind leaves the door unlocked?"

She giggled. "Just one little action sets off a series of events. The gods are quite clever. They once got me a free lunch at McDonald's. Someone had left their food behind in a rush..."

I kept going, not wanting to hear her talk about eating food some stranger had touched.

We walked through the foyer, across perfectly polished oak floors, towards the hallway leading away from a great room. My gaze flicked about, searching for signs of life, but there wasn't much. This scene could've been plucked from a home decor magazine. What was missing were the personal touches though. No family photos. No knick-knacks or memories from travel.

A bookcase next to the stone fireplace held many books —as well as Betsy Lee DuMaire's paperbacks.

"What does she write?" I asked.

"Romantic thrillers." Abby shivered. "The books aren't too graphic, but when the scenes run through Betsy Lee's head they're so disturbing..."

A thud from the right corner of the house caught my attention.

"I hear pups," I said. "Maybe kids?"

"Yeah, Betsy Lee has five of them. I never see them when I'm here."

Dodging one adult wasn't too hard, but five kids invited landmines.

From the hallway we reached the kitchen. And that's where the fantasy home ended. Gorgeous sandstone-colored quartz countertops were buried under abandoned cups, crusty food-covered plates, and crayon drawings of a dog dressed like a doctor. And that was just the counters. Right next to the stainless steel fridge, a mountain of empty TV dinner boxes littered the overwhelmed trash bin.

"Can this chick afford a maid?" I managed.

"I don't know. I never saw one while I was here."

"And what happened to this table?" I ran my hand along what looked like a werewolf-sized bite on the side. "Do they let the kids out at night to feed them?"

"Oh, Nat...c'mon."

I snickered. "Uncle Boris got drunk during the full moon once and used the side of my aunt's kitchen table as a scratching post. Aunt Vera kicked his ass for days afterward."

Beyond the kitchen, we headed deeper into the house.

At this point, I was ready to glimpse a disheveled, braless woman snacking on gummy bears. Not everyone is as tidy as I am, but geez, she has kids in the house.

Past the kitchen, another hallway took us to a sun room converted into an office. Abby kept going while I darted around the corner. A peek was all I'd needed to leave me floored. A tall figure sat at the computer playing Guild Wars. That figure wasn't what I expected.

Betsy Lee is a dude. Houston, the erratic rocket has lifted off.

Abby's footsteps were barely perceptible with all the battle sound effects coming from the game. She was getting closer. Unable to quench my curiosity, I looked around the corner again. A familiar smell reached my nose. The same sweet scent of cinnamon my therapist had.

Also, Betsy Lee is the pseudonym of a *warlock*.

One of the deadliest foe's a werewolf can encounter. Back when I'd made a trip into Atlantic City to save my brother, I met one who killed others for cold, hard cash. A pulse of fear raced up my legs just remembering the power emanating from him. The wolf within me forced me to crouch low. *Run*, it urged, but I didn't bolt.

Abby was right next to him, but the man didn't acknowledge her. Abby gave a knowing smile and touched Betsy Lee's shoulder as if to comfort him. Her charge still didn't react.

If something happened, I'd make a run for it and I was dragging her with me. Book be damned.

Then Abby deftly looked behind the desktop unit and followed the cord to the router. With a single touch, the Internet fell over and died.

Betsy Lee cursed. "Oh, c'mon, I was almost to the Gate of Madness!"

He slammed his fist on the desk while Abby threw me a wink. "Ugh! What I wouldn't give for a fucking Internet spell." With his precious connection gone, Betsy Lee ended the program leaving only one application left: his word processor.

"I guess this piece of shit story isn't going to write itself," he grumbled. "Time to off some folks."

FOR THE NEXT HALF HOUR, I watched Abby work her magic. Not once did the warlock turn around and notice me. Couldn't he sense me?

My heart was beating fast enough for me to run down a bunch of ornaments in a discount aisle.

Seeing a warlock and a muse write a book together was rather creepy—but amazing, too. A feared spellcaster was typing away at a romantic suspense novella while Abby kept him on task.

Then I caught the sounds of movement from the kitchen. I glanced around to see potential places for me to hide. I didn't have too many options. Either stuff myself into the hall closet across from the office or hide in the washing machine in the laundry room one door down.

But no one came and they made all sorts of noise shifting through the crap on the kitchen counters. Curious to see who I'd need to dodge, I did some reconnaissance. Might as well see if there's a few little witches and warlocks roaming about.

I darted down the hallway, stopping every now and

then to listen. Once I reached the wall leading to the kitchen, I leaned down and peeked around the corner—not the easiest task in a pencil skirt and low heels.

Two blond kids, one as tall as one of my middle-schooler cousins was searching through the fridge. Another child who looked about five or six waited beside her brother.

The fact that the girl wore a pink skirt and pineapple pajama bottoms wasn't really what caught my attention.

It was the sad state of the refrigerator. In a house like this one, with a state-of-the-art appliance I could *never* afford, there was barely a damn thing to eat. No fresh food. Just mystery Tupperware containers and old pizza boxes.

The boy glanced inside, gave up, and then went straight for a wallet hidden under a pile of papers.

Was he seriously going to steal from his dad?

I watched in awe as the kid took out a credit card.

"Aww, Mike!" the little girl complained. "I don't want pizza again. It makes my tummy upset."

The boy shrugged. "I'll get you a salad again."

"Ew. Mommy wouldn't make me eat that..."

I concur. Most pizza places didn't do salads well.

"Just stop it, Carrie," the boy replied. "There's nothing else."

"Can't we walk to the store again?"

I closed my eyes and prayed for Abby to show up so I could drag her author in here. Two kids walking over five miles on a country road? What the hell?

"We can't use the credit card in the store," Mike explained.

"What about a spell?" Carrie asked.

"I tried to make spaghetti and it came alive and *ate* a part of the kitchen table."

So that's what happened...

My wizard friend Nick told me creating food was very hard for spellcasters. I guess these kids never got that memo.

Carrie giggled. "At least dad stopped working to kill it."

The kids turned around so I found my hiding spot again. They walked across the room and I heard the sound of a dial tone and someone hitting buttons. The young warlock mumbled faint words under his breath, and then spoke.

"Yeah, I'd like to order a pizza, please." Mike's voice now sounded like a barrel-chested lumberjack on speed. If he couldn't get that right, the likelihood I'd get caught by them was quite low.

Once the pizza was ordered the kids left the kitchen, leaving me alone to ponder my life and how I seemed to keep following trouble around.

It was only a late Friday afternoon and a set of complete strangers traipsed through these poor kids' home. Instead of letting the wood floor hold me up, I explored parts of the house. I'd only have so long before the pizza showed up. I'd need a place to stay tonight. Hanging out in the office near the creepy warlock wasn't gonna happen.

Betsy Lee's master suite was on the ground floor. Compared to the living room, this space looked like a home. Between two grand windows along the far wall, a large framed family painting added a splash of color. Five smiling kids—three boys and two girls—surrounded two blond adults. They looked like any other family standing in front of their house on a beautiful summer day.

Even I cracked a smile at the sight.

Growing up, I hadn't encountered too many warlocks.

I'd met plenty of witches. Now that I was older though, the bad apples kept falling off the tree. It was far too easy to recall the bad people who made the good ones look bad. My history with spellcasters had left me feeling wary, but maybe meeting a run-of-the-mill family would be good for me.

A fresh start.

I sighed, thinking of Nick. I'd never asked him about his life growing up. Did he have a family like this one? I looked at the painting again. Where was the witch now? Were they divorced? Where had she gone? Had she died? Maybe she had abandoned them?

Just the very thought dampened my mood.

A half hour later, the pizza arrived and a herd of hungry kids invaded the kitchen. I had no place to go so I found a spot in the master bedroom's walk-in closet on the carpeted floor. As I sat there, I couldn't stop myself from laughing my ass off.

Here I was, sitting on the floor with pressed pants hanging over my head and I was hiding from spellcasters that normally trap werewolves for nefarious spells.

I came here willingly...for a friend. Beyond the closet, a window offered an escape path. I could peel out of here and sleep in a nice normal hotel room.

And yet I stayed and closed my eyes for a quick nap. Abby had work to do and it looked like I had some as well.

CHAPTER 4

I'D NEVER THOUGHT the day would come when I could say I'd slept in a warlock's home, but it happened. A good five-hour long power nap did me good. I stretched and my empty stomach growled on cue. When the full moon loomed, the local buffets turned into werewolf hang outs.

As much as I loved sanitary eating conditions, I wouldn't have turned a filthy buffet down right about now. And I could smell the pizza the kids got. A quick glance at my watch showed 10 P.M. Would they be asleep? At least the younger ones?

I snuck out of the master suite to the kitchen. Thankfully, the lights were out. And, of course, nothing had been put away. Two open pizza boxes sat on the heap.

My mind screamed *no* while my stomach cried out *hell yes.* The remaining pizza, if you could call it that, consisted of greasy slices with curly, burnt ends.

What kind of slop was that to feed kids? Ugh! Humans definitely made pizza better than werewolves, but some establishments were better off for massive bonfires than buffets.

I was starving, but I hadn't reached desperate yet.

And poor Carrie hadn't touched her salad. The takeout container with the meal sat on the kitchen table. At least a few buffalo wings had been nibbled on.

Instead of giving in to my empty stomach, I peeked in on Abby and Betsy Lee. Abby's charge was working away furiously at the pages. Abby glanced at me and I motioned for her to come to the hallway.

"No," she mouthed. "I'm on the job."

I feigned a growl and motioned harder for her to come to me. The girl-I'm-not-playing expression I gave probably worked. She left Betsy Lee's side and the author faltered for a moment, but kept going at a slower pace.

Good. Maybe he'd remember to feed his kids and take a shower. I could smell him from the other side of the house.

"What's wrong?" Abby whispered. Her voice was so soft I barely heard it.

"What's wrong?" I gestured around us. "Have you seen this house?"

She didn't even blink. "Yeah, I had to help her finish her last thriller a year ago. That plot line was sooooo creepy."

I tilted my head. "Her? Isn't Betsy Lee a guy?"

"I know that, but I'm used to saying her..."

I rolled my eyes. "The kitchen is unfit for kids."

"And?" She took a step back toward Betsy Lee.

"What about the empty fridge? You ever looked in there?"

"Not really." Abby added distance between us, forcing me to follow her back into the office. "I don't eat when I work."

I sucked in my lips. *Wow, it's like that, huh?*

"So you show up to work and everything else around you is ignored?" I whispered with a hiss.

She sighed. Her arm reached behind her toward what really mattered to her: Betsy Lee. "It's not like that. If we were in danger, I'd let you know."

"I'm talking about the *kids*, Abby. Do you come here for every assignment and just watch them get neglected?"

Her stony face faltered for a moment and I almost regretted putting her on the spot like that.

I crossed my arms. I was done here. "I'm going out. Do you want anything?"

She shook her head, a decision made as she touched Betsy Lee and spurned her author to write like mad again.

I didn't look back as I snuck out the door to the patio. Neither Betsy Lee nor Abby heard me leave.

Maybe they didn't care.

Two hours later, I got back to the house after navigating through the minuscule grocery store in Dryer. South Toms River at least had the Stop & Shop Supermarket. That place wasn't as large as A&P or Wal-mart, but it had more than the shop in Dryer.

Now that I had the goods, I had to deal with the fun part: Getting this shit into the house.

A quick glance through the kitchen window revealed a room with a single occupant: the youngest girl, Carrie.

She sat at the kitchen table poking at that sad-looking salad. Good kid. At least she hadn't given up.

Just when I thought Carrie planned to eat the food, she looked about, then whispered over her meal. A second or two later the lettuce twitched, and then as if it had a mind of its own, her dinner tried to make a run for it. Carrie grabbed the nearest dirty plastic cup.

"Die!" she yelled. After a few good hits from her mighty mug, the pesky food moved no more.

I sighed, happy I grew up in a household where our food stayed put.

I didn't have to wait long for Carrie to turn off the light and leave the kitchen. Once the sounds of her footsteps faded toward the kids' rooms, I entered the house through the front door and quickly carried the grocery bags into the kitchen.

I tried to be quiet, but the plastic bags made too much noise as I grabbed fruit and slid old Tupperware containers across the ceramic tile floor towards the trash pile.

I made great progress—the fruit and vegetable drawer had actual fruit—until something moved along the edge of my peripheral vision.

Carrie's salad, or perhaps I should say what used to be her salad, slithered across the floor towards my foot. Inch by inch, the lettuce legs propelled the creature my way. Crouton eyes focused on me. Its slime trail led from under the table across the floor.

Now that is wrong on so many levels. Now I got veggie roaches...

I hurried to finish unloading the bags. Task complete, I turned around to see Carrie looking at me.

That sneaky kid had tricked even my keen werewolf hearing.

"Hey." What else could I say? I was a stranger in her house.

"You have to smash it a few more times," she said softly.

"*What?*"

"That." She pointed at the slimy salad that was determined to go for my foot again.

"Oh, yeah." I dug my right heel into the lumpiest part of

the salad. After a few hearty stabs, the sentient salad was quiet again.

After that I waited for her to speak. Maybe scream bloody murder, but she just stared at me.

"Are you Daddy's new assistant?" she asked.

"No...I'm Natalya. I'm his assistant's *assistant*." I'd say chauffeur, but things were already weird. "You're Carrie, right?"

She nodded. "I guess you're not here to take care of us. A few years ago when Mommy and Daddy lived together, we had a lady who helped." She smiled and my heart broke. "Before Mommy left last year, things were different."

"I'm sure they were."

The salad twitched so Carrie kicked it into a corner. "I'm hungry." She looked at me expectantly.

Was I supposed to do something?

She stepped around me and opened the fridge. "Ohhh, juice boxes and Lunchables. The good kind." She plucked a portable kid snack from the stack I left. I watched with suspicion as she searched the countertops for a plate. With her forearm, she tried to brush off a purple plastic plate with hardened pizza sauce on one side *and* discolored peanut butter on the other.

I shuddered, unable to take it anymore.

"Stop!" I hissed.

I snatched the soiled plate and gave her a few paper towels instead. "Just use that."

"But I don't eat these without a plate." She presented her lunch meat squares and cheese with a dead serious face.

Since Carrie was determined to have a plate, I set about doing the dishes. I knew where this was going and what was about to happen, but I had to let it go and release the OCD Kraken so to speak. Armed with every disinfectant I could find under the sink, I washed the dishes, wiped down the floor, and tossed the empty boxes into the recycle bin in the garage. The squirmy salad might not have disappeared, but at least the kitchen was clean and Carrie had a plate for her snack.

Now that she ate and the room smelled like antiseptic heaven, a peaceful feeling settled over me, but this little victory wouldn't last as long as it took the kids to dirty every dish and empty the fridge.

~

When I woke up in the walk-in closet on Saturday morning, my weekend was halfway over.

I'd used a dapper black suitcoat as my pillow and a light-blue bathrobe as a blanket. My late night shower had helped me relax, but now every muscle in my back was stiff from sleeping curled up in the corner.

Not once did the warlock visit his bedroom to sleep. His work continued to consume him.

Now that I'd run into Carrie, I gave up sneaking around and headed to the kids' rooms. A stray sweater in the middle of the hallway was the first hint I'd found the right place. Another few feet down the hall, a Monopoly game—with all the pieces and money in place—sat ready. Did anyone put anything away in this house?

Four doorways led to rooms. In the first room I spotted a familiar face. Carrie, along with a mountain of tiny plastic dolls, was stretched out on her eldest brother's double bed while Mike was in the other corner sketching on an artist's workbench.

He glanced at me with suspicion.

"Hey, Natalya," Carrie said.

"Who are you?" Mike asked. He looked like he was about to get up. Even though he wasn't that big, it was nice to see *someone* around here wanted to take care of things.

"This is the lady who brought all the food last night. She works for daddy."

"Thanks," Mike said gruffly.

Carrie motioned me over. She had on a different shirt, but the same skirt and pajama bottoms. "Want to play Fashion Witch Dream Rescue? I'll be the bad witch if you wanna be the good one."

I offered her a smile. "Uh, I'm good."

Mike's room was pretty big. Betsy Lee had invested a pretty penny for a home this large on the countryside. Dark blue walls might've damped the room's mood, but the numerous windows let in so much light. On the opposite side of the expansive room, a corner was filled with bookcases and books. Many of them I recognized as educational materials. *Field's Manual for Budding Spellcasters* to *Know Your Wood: Your Magic Wand and You.*

The books had dust on them. Not surprised.

He kept a pretty clean space for a boy. Growing up, my brother's room should've had an "enter at your own risk" sign. You could smell the funk through the closed door. He was pretty cool for letting his little sister play in here.

Without seeming too obvious, I tried to see what he was working on. Most shoppers at The Bends disliked having a clerk looking over their shoulder, too, so I walked around until I had the best angle to peek at what Mike drew. I expected perhaps an anime character or something—not a replica of the portrait I saw on the wall in Betsy Lee's bedroom. I had to clench my fists from saying something out loud. For goodness sake, these kids needed a freakin' parent.

To keep myself in check, I spoke. "You have a lot of books, Mike. Do you have to study magic?"

"Not as much as I should," he replied. "I want to study in NYC someday and go to school like other warlocks."

My hackles were raised further. Did that mean...?

"Do you go to school?" I asked Carrie.

"No, we're homeschooled," Mike said for her.

Which means no. "Who teaches you?"

Mike shrugged. "Mom used to teach us, but now Dad does it."

I snorted. "When does that happen?"

"When he finds time..." Mike's voice faded a bit. "I'm the one who teaches now."

Oh, God, that's why these kids couldn't cast a spell. "Umm, Mike, no more spellcasting on the food. Sooner or later you're gonna create something you can't handle."

He shrugged. "We try our best."

"I know you do—which is why I'm offering a hand while I'm here. Your dad has an important story to finish." I motioned for him to keep drawing.

While he worked on the sketch of his family, I couldn't help thinking about growing up with my parents. No matter how many crazy things went down, my loud overwhelming Russian family was somewhat *stable*. They were also present.

Even with my brief shunning from the pack last year, I managed to get my life back on track.

What chance did these kids have now? Would they grow up and not know their father since he was determined to find oblivion with his words? Watching their father hard at work unnerved me in other ways: Was this what I was like when I was obsessed with something? Would I be like this if my mental illness worsened?

For the rest of the day, I followed Carrie around. Abby never left the office. Even when I brought a tray of two bowls of soup and two coffees, only one person had touched the food. My friend never moved from her place by his side, which meant her author had eaten.

I mean, who would want working conditions like this. The last time I'd checked on them, Betsy Lee had been working on a flashback scene where the hero's wife had been murdered.

Okay, I will admit the writing was vivid with details that shoved me headfirst into the story, but Abby had to see the scene before Betsy Lee put it down on paper.

Like a good friend, I left some of the pot roast dinner I cooked the kids on a tray outside the door. I didn't expect Abby to eat again.

I spent the night in Carrie's Pepto-Bismol pink room. That way I could at least make sure she took a bath and changed clothes. The little kid couldn't cast spells to save her life, but she was quite talented at building blanket forts. And, well, if you have a werewolf who can lift heavy stuff, you can make some pretty cool structures.

The next morning I woke up with Carrie lying next to me. The house was quiet and the sounds of kids snoring in other rooms reached my ears. The whole scene was serene —until something moved across my foot. I leaned my head up to peek.

The slimy green salad thing was *nibbling* on my toes.

And there was more than one of them.

I sucked in a very long breath. At least today was Sunday.

How many times had Carrie tried to fix her food? There had to be five of those things wiggling on me. After I made a few good kicks, the creatures ended up hiding among the toys in her room.

I looked into the fort at Carrie. I couldn't go without saying goodbye to the sleepy-eyed kiddo. She stirred a bit after I got up.

"It was great meeting you," I whispered to her. "I have to take your dad's assistant...back to New York."

"Okay." She smiled a bit and then turned off to go back to sleep.

That gesture she made saddened me even further.

The poor girl was used to not having anyone stay for long. I wanted to hug her—something I rarely did with strangers—but I didn't. She needed her dad to take care of her.

I lingered at the door. That was the most I could do.

CHAPTER 5

THE FULL MOON loomed and it was time for me to go home and hunt with my pack tonight.

When I approached the office, the room was dead quiet. The typing had ceased and only Betsy Lee's even breaths could be heard.

I found the muse crouched in the corner, her eyes glassy and distant. Her once glossy brown hair was now dull and disheveled.

Had she rested at all?

Betsy Lee was fast asleep with his head resting on the keyboard. The words, 'The End' lay at the end of a beautiful page.

I stooped in front of Abby as Betsy Lee began to snore.

"How you doing?" I touched the side of her face and found her skin was cold.

"The story is done." She smiled weakly. "The hero got revenge for his murdered wife and now he can make a new start with the woman who helped him. My author *finished* her book on time."

"Looks like he did."

I helped Abby up. She was exhausted, but the next step wasn't mine to take. "You're not done yet, kiddo."

"What do you mean?" she asked.

"I'm not giving you a ride home until you help your author fix his *life*."

Her eyebrow furrowed. "His life is fine. This next story will be amazing."

"Oh, wake up..."

She crossed her arms. "I have boundaries, Nat."

"Yes, let's pretend nothing's wrong and do nothing. Like you said a few days ago, you can't change anything. You're going to see the same horrible shit over and over again." I advanced on her to make my frustration clear. "Heidi has *let* you do these little gigs like this because it's *easy*. It's easy to walk in, do your job, and leave. What if you could really use your gift to do more?"

"What do you want me to do?" A tear slid down her cheek. "I'm in pieces here."

I wiped it away. She wasn't gonna get a hug like a pup. "You said your gift is that you can be at the right place at the right time for your authors. I know you're shaken up right now, but you can do *even* more than Betsy Lee. What you saw in his head isn't real. This room, this man, those kids. They're real. Believe in that."

I squeezed her arm, and then left the house. It was up to Abby to make this next choice. That was one of the first things Dr. Frank had taught us: we had the power to do more with our lives and not repeat the same undesired behaviors.

I wasn't sure how long I waited for Abby, but it was long enough for me to advance through five levels of Candy Crush. And I somehow managed to run out of time and made the candy bombs go off without trying.

While I waited I also made a decision. If Abby couldn't help them, I would call Child Protective Services. I wasn't sure how they'd react showing up to a supernatural home, but that wasn't for me to decide.

I was in the middle of my sixth game when I saw Abby through the living room window. Squinting to the point my forehead hurt, I watched the muse place something in her hand on the floor next to the couch.

She left the house, and then turned to face the doorway. A moment later she picked up the doormat and flipped it on its side. What the heck was she doing?

My game long forgotten, I stared her down until she smiled at me. A sly, slow grin from the woman who hopefully did me proud.

"You did it?" I asked.

She nodded. "I did."

I started the car. We drove for a bit and the gooey feeling inside of me increased. Carrie's life would be better now—but in what way?

We were a half hour into the ride when I gave in. "I gotta know. What the hell were you doing?"

"I usually depend on the gods to guide my path, but this time I *helped* a bit. You ever heard of a Rube Goldberg machine?"

"Yeah, aren't those contraptions fit together to do a task? A bunch of unnecessary contraptions to do one simple thing?"

She nodded.

"So you setup one?" I asked.

She rolled down the window and a gentle breeze brought the forest to my nose. Tonight would be a good run. A good day to be a werewolf.

Her expression turned wistful. "On a sunny day like

this one, the kitchen window will be open. A bird will lightly land on the piece of bread left on the windowsill. As it takes the food, it will knock over a small cup. That cup will roll across the kitchen and bump into this little slimy thing crawling across the floor..."

I chuckled, thinking of these events taking place.

Abby continued. "Now that Betsy Lee is done with her book, she will go to sleep for a while, but when she wakes up she'll walk across the living room and see the gift I left for her there. A picture of her family her eldest drew for her. Betsy Lee thinks about pictures when she misses...When *he* misses his wife. That photo was taken in front of his house and is now a painting on his wall." She paused. "If that bird falls in just the right place, soon enough Betsy Lee will be standing outside with his face in the sun and his mind on his family instead of his work."

Wonderful. "Good job, Abby."

"Thanks."

I had to ask. "So, umm, what happens if a bird doesn't take the bread?"

Abby sighed and rolled her eyes. "Betsy Lee will trip on the cup and his kids will call an ambulance. They'll end up happily ever after because he'll break his hand."

I laughed and smiled for the next mile and a half. Now that story seemed more likely...

The End

NEVER BET ON A SUCCUBUS

*Reader Note: This story, from Heidi the mermaid's
perspective, takes place before Coveted (Coveted #1)*

"There's no way in hell I'm letting you walk out of this
apartment wearing that." Not that I could say much since I
was a mermaid giving fashion advice to a soul-sucking
succubus, but I had to say something. I eyed Lilith's coat
with distaste. "The pimp you stole that coat from wants it
back. Now."

Lilith's pale face stretched into a grimace. She clutched
the over-sized, fur-bearing lapel closer as if I'd snatch it
away. That wasn't happening. Even if it was a designer
label.

"It's not that bad..." At my side, my cohort in action,
Abby, tried to sound enthusiastic. She wasn't as convincing
since her voice trailed off to a whisper.

I switched on the overhead lights in Lilith's cramped
living room. A bit smaller than most in New York City's
East Village neighborhood. Maybe a bit more lighting—
other than the lamp in the corner—would make Lilith's

outfit look better. I quickly flicked the light back off. Nope. Didn't help. In the light, Lilith's features were front and center for the world to see. I've met succubi before, and none of them looked as broke down as she did. Instead of long, willowy legs, Lilith had knobby knees and thicker calves. Her bright orange dress, which *hardly* hit mid-thigh, had a lopsided hemline and fit her like a potato sack. Her curves were non-existent, though based on past experience, I knew she shot straight down like puberty had been an afterthought.

I had a better chance of taking down a pirate ship during calm weather. I cast a glare at Abby. Why did I place a bet with the Muse again?

"I'm not taking back my bet," Abby chirped.

Fuck, I hated when it felt like she read my mind. I'd asked her once if her race was telepathic, and she told me she was good at reading people. "I have to understand what my authors need," she'd said. "When it comes to everyone else, including other supernatural creatures, it's all about intuition." Which meant she saw through my antics like a bad check.

"In less than twenty-four hours, you need to get her a date or else you have to take a stroll into the Atlantic ocean. At least up to your knees," Abby said firmly.

A mean bet to make with someone who hadn't gone into the ocean in over a decade. All the ladies in the room attended my therapy group. We all had issues. Mine in particular were geographic in nature. I didn't go near large bodies of water anymore. Looking at the sea or smelling it at times left me anxious and on edge. The Muse, Abby, had issues after all the years she'd peered into her authors' heads. In particular, the thriller and horror authors she constantly had to handle. Today, thanks to working with a motivational author who wrote about his jaunts to Amsterdam to find himself in the cannabis coffee shops, Abby handled herself quite well. I, on the other hand, predicted doom.

"We need to change her clothes," I whispered to Abby.

"You promised you'd let her try to dress herself. Like a big girl."

I gestured to the Florida orange in front of us. "I think this is an epic fail here. The Spice Girls are walking around naked right now."

"They're not a band anymore," Abby pointed out.

"'Cause Lilith stole their wardrobe!" I said.

"If this isn't working," Lilith said crisply, "then what should I wear? I'm ready and willing to get a good man tonight."

Her eagerness made me uneasy. While Abby went through the backup-bag, as I called it, I asked Lilith, "When was the last time you ate?"

"I had a club sandwich for lunch—"

"I mean *eat*. As in a succubus meal?"

She shrugged. "I had drive-thru a few days ago."

Drive-through soul-sucking? When she caught my puzzled expression, she said, "There's a shop on East 24th where people who want to make a quick buck—"

"—I don't want to know," I sputtered. Why couldn't people just donate blood like the good ol' days when they needed a few bucks? "Either way, you're not allowed to eat anyone. No nibbling, no soul-crunching, driving-through-ing, whatever the hell you do, it's not permitted tonight. You got it?"

"I promise." Her smile was smug.

Thirst tickled my senses. An ever-present need since I lived on land. Time for a refill. As I downed a liter of water

I tried to muster up some confidence. I made a promise, and if that meant I had to dress up Lilith and put some make-up on her and strut her around East Village in front of my inebriated friends until she got some digits, I'd do what I had to do. There was no way in hell I was setting a foot in East River or the Hudson either. I'd seen too much weird shit floating around in there.

Abby tossed Lilith a classic red dress and black pumps. "The color red signifies she's ready to copulate," Abby said proudly.

The dress did help. Compared to the last ensemble, this one showed how tiny her waist was. A plus. She even looked a bit better than the Muse, who for some reason tended to stick to the color brown. She wore a pair of fitted brown shorts and a halter top. Her legs were long and slim. She'd have no problems getting attention. The ones who'd be able to see her anyway. Only the authors Muses inspired could see them and other supernatural creatures like Lilith and myself.

"Next, make-up," I declared.

"I already have some on," Lilith said.

"And now you're taking that off."

After Lilith removed her circus make-up, I added the final touch. A bit of foundation and lip-gloss. After she saw my handy work, Lilith made a face. "We're getting you a man tonight, right?" I reminded her.

"A man. One with a pulse."

"That's the spirit!" I added.

I washed my hands and checked myself in the mirror before we left. The last thing I needed was to go out with make-up smeared all over myself. My camouflage tube dress was fitted in all the right places. Revealing for the twins on top and clingy for the curvy hips down low. If I had to be the fish bait to snag her a man, I'd do it. I was the official wingman tonight.

"Let's get me a man," Lilith cheered.

By the end of the night, I'd regret her words.

"So this is the last place where you got close?" Abby asked. She peered at the flashing lights above a night club entrance off East 9th and 2nd Ave.

Back when I'd lived in the sea, I'd lived as a soldier so I'd planned this out like any other battle. First step, choose the location wisely. I could head to any of the bars in Soho or the Lower East Side. Shit, there were probably eager men waiting in Brooklyn who wanted to give her a good time. But, the way I saw it, why not first try the place she got close to scoring last time? Maybe it was a bar full of blind dudes.

The thumps from the music's bass inside reverberated into my arms and legs. My kind of place already. The line outside was pretty long. Mostly guys and a few girls hanging out and talking. A nicely dressed black man, with a bouncer standing next to him, took their money as they filed inside. We headed for the end of the line.

"Hey ladies," the man called out to us. He didn't even bother looking into my eyes. Just one long look at my thighs down to my leather boots. If he only knew what my legs *really* looked like he might be passed out on the floor.

"What's up?" I said.

"You pretty ladies want in?" he asked.

"Sure." Abby handed me the cash, and I stepped forward to pay. Her bet, her cash.

I'd asked her once how muses made money. It wasn't

like she could get a regular job since humans couldn't see her. All she did was give me a sly wink. "I get tips."

I didn't want to elaborate further. Especially since it led to me thinking my best friend got her pocket change from offering additional *services* to her authors.

Lilith was all smiles. A much more jovial mood than the times in group therapy where she was trying to cop a feel on the male members while she complained about any and everything.

If I remembered right, her last complaint was: "The last time I was close to a man in bed was at the hospital during visiting hours."

The bouncer opened the door and we rushed inside. It was so packed, there were human bodies practically gyrating in the hallway toward the lit dance floor. Pulse-pounding dub-step music hit my ears. The whole space was decorated like a glitter bomb—filled with streamer guts and balloon innards—had exploded. We'd apparently arrived at a great time. I flashed Abby a grin. We'd be out of here soon. The opposite sex filled every corner. Men in casual clothes to ones in suits and ties. A select few without shirts. Very nice.

But one thing was painfully obvious as we stirred through the crowd in search of the tables toward the rear. I didn't see a lot of women. And most of the men were gorgeous, too. I didn't need to be a mermaid with keen eyesight to spot tight asses and abs like chiseled stone. Practically delectable like sushi. But there should be other women here too, hunting like we were. A lone blonde danced with a group of men, while a tall, leggy redhead did shots with other men at the bar. My eyes flitted around the room, counting like I was on a battleground looking for enemies. As we flowed through the crowd, a lot of men danced—with other men—but many of them were perfectly willing to have women join them.

We reached an empty table and even Abby knew what was up. "No wonder she thought she was scoring."

Instead of continuing to count past the fifteen women I'd spotted, I hunted for a waiter instead. I'd need some liquor and a jug of water to survive tonight. Probably a lot more water than liquor to keep from getting dehydrated.

Damn, the men here looked so good. And most of them were playing for the other team. I watched with fascination as one guy danced with another, his hands roaming across a wide back, then down to grip his dance partner's narrow hips. Their heads were tilted away so I couldn't see it, but my mind filled in the blanks as they shared a deep kiss...

"Yo, Heidi!" Abby tapped me on the shoulder. Then on the head. "I can tell you need a drink. You're getting pale."

"I'm already pale," I murmured. One woman, apparently out with friends, was sandwiched between three guys, giggling and shaking her ass. Holy shit, I want to be a sandwich like that. Any kind didn't matter. I was an equal opportunity filler.

"Lilith, tell the waiter we want a pitcher of water and a rum and Coke. Light on the ice." Abby had been out with me far too often.

"What are you doing?" Abby asked me.

"I'm fulfilling my part of the bet," I said seriously. "I'm looking for a man for her."

"I don't think most of the men here are looking for what she's got. She's missing—"

"—how do you know?" I blurted. "There's women here. There might be a few straight guys peppered in here."

"I doubt it."

"So you're saying gay guys don't have straight friends?"

She crossed her arms. "I'm just saying the possibility of finding the kind of man she wants here will be a bit hard."

"I'd love some bright ideas, then. How about we go to a church service with a minor-demon succubus or hunt down quality men at the local coffee shop? I hate to break the news flash to you, but the lighting here is poor and those guys just want to have fun. I doubt they're trying to get Double D over there into bed." I jerked my head toward the blonde whose tits bounced around like two basketballs were trying to free themselves from a bag.

"So what happened last time?" I asked Lilith.

"I came in on Saturday, like today, and I had a few drinks. Not long after midnight, I was dancing with a bunch of guys." She had a glint in her eyes that sadly resembled a hungry chick waiting in line at the buffet.

"That sounds good," I said. "Time for you to do it again. This time, single out a guy if he shows interest."

"How can she tell—" Abby asked.

"We're building up confidence here. A warm up." I hoped.

Lilith didn't need to be asked. She darted out.

I grabbed her arm. "Oh, uh, Lilith, could you look less like I'm-hungry-for-your-soul and more come-hither-and-fuck-me?"

She nodded profusely. "That I can do!"

"Go, get 'em, Tiger!" I pushed her into the crowd. "*Rawr!*"

This was gonna be good. Once on the floor, Lilith strutted her stuff. Almost a jerk-like motion where her limbs bent and flexed like she was convulsing. A couple, having a good time, quickly got out of her way to give her room. A lot of it.

"Go, Lilith!" Abby yelled.

I filled my glass with water and downed it. The liquor was next. Lilith's jerky motion dance turned into some kind of hip-hop dance gone wrong. I tossed back the shot glass. Damn, I was gonna need more.

"I need to go through the crowd," I said to Abby. "See if I can find someone who parties for Team Heterosexual. Shit, even Team Bisexual is welcome. Did Lilith say she was willing to date a woman?"

"She's only mentioned men," Abby replied. "Although I've yet to see a succubus turn down either sex for a meal."

"Good point."

I strolled through the crowd, stretching across sweaty bodies and easing past hot men. It was hard not to be pulled toward them. Almost like an invisible line tugged me in their direction, beckoning me to let my hair loose and move with them. Suddenly, there were hands on my hips, hands on my shoulders. I flowed with the pulsing music, shaking and grinding, bobbing my head to the beat.

"Work it, girl!" one man yelled.

And work it, I did.

In the haze induced by the dancers, thoughts swam around in my head. Wasn't I supposed to be doing some-thing right now? Scoping out men? One sexy man closed in front of me, his hips moving in time to the beat. He was good. My red hair fell out of my topknot, and I lost myself to the music. I was just one with the mass of bodies. One of the dancers flowing with the music. Whistles and cat calls filled the air. Sweat mingled with sweat. The faint scent of pot from someone who'd taken several generous drags before he entered the bar. I gripped skin, heated and firm. They had no idea I was no mere woman, but that didn't matter. Only the moment.

Until I caught the dirty look from the muse across the

room. Her arms were crossed and her brown eyes cast a fish net of venom my way.

I mouthed, "I was scoping out men."

"Uh huh," she replied.

I left the tangle of bodies and spotted Lilith at the bar.

Time to get back to work.

CHAPTER 2

LILITH MOPED AT THE BAR. Her attempts to buy a guy a drink didn't look too good. After she pushed the drink in his direction, he shook his head and pushed it back. Even with the roar of the music, I focused enough to hear him spout, "I'm not that drunk. Just 'cause you're in drag doesn't mean I'm interested."

Wow. He wasn't even that good looking either. *Jerk!*

I marched over to them. He looked me over and murmured, "hey," when I squeezed myself between them. Let's see if he could take what he dished out to others.

"Did you find someone?" I whined to Lilith loud enough for the asshole to hear. "I'm not having another three-way again unless we find someone who's willing to let me give them non-stop blow jobs and spankings."

Lilith stared at me as if I'd gleefully taken a dip in the East River. I took the lemon drop martini he rejected, downed it in a single gulp, then I licked the sugar off the edge, my tongue sliding down the glass using suggestive flicks. The man watched the whole time, mouth agape. *Take that, fucker!*

"What's your name?" he asked me.

"We're a package deal, Sweetie. Too bad you missed out." I laced my arm around Lilith's and left the bar.

She reluctantly followed. "He was interested," she hissed. "I could practically taste how hard his—"

"Not worth it. He wanted us as a package deal not you alone."

"I wouldn't mind a three-way."

I snorted. "The bet was a date for you, not a porn video."

Lilith followed me as I went around the tables, checking to see if a new target came my way. It didn't take me long to catch the gaze of a man staring at me. He sat with a bunch of other guys. There were a few couples at the table, some of them gay. He was the only one checking me out, and the other women in the other room. Bingo.

"Lilith," I whispered in her ear. "I want you to go dance." I pointed to the spot where a group of guys were dancing with some girls. Lilith would stand out, not in the best way, but at least my pitch would show she was trying to have a good time.

After Lilith left my side, I headed to the table, making sure to pull my hair back into a messy topknot and yank down the hem of my dress. I wasn't on the menu tonight.

Almost everyone at the table looked up when I approached.

"Michael, it looks like one of the ladies spotted you," one man on the end said, his arm around his date.

Michael, a brown-haired guy who had the rough looks of a younger Keanu Reeves, grinned at me. He had an adorable over-bite, but he'd work for tonight.

A few guys slid out so I could take a seat next to Michael. It was a tight squeeze, but we all fit. Michael didn't look too bad now that I was closer. But he had a smell deep under his skin that immediately turned me off. The sea lingered under his fingernails and permeated from him. Not that he didn't wash or anything. To a human nose he was crisp and clean. But I had a nose as good as a shark's. Michael worked as a fisherman, or even more likely, as someone who got his pay from working on a boat. The very thought made my stomach churn. He wasn't for me though, I reminded myself.

We introduced ourselves to each other. Might as well get the small talk out of the way.

"See my friend over there?" I pointed to the succubus trying to bust a move and do the robot to techno-music. "It's her birthday tonight and she could really use a hero."

After sharing a drink, and some polite conversation with Michael, I managed to convince him to be nice to the not-quite-birthday girl. Thank the shifty underworld gods I didn't have to go further into my lie and tell him something outlandish like she had testicular cancer.

I slid out of the booth with Michael following me. I didn't have to nudge him or anything. He simply walked up to her and asked to dance. He kept a healthy distance, though, from her flying fists. He tried to do his own thing without cramping her style. After a while, I even caught him laughing. At our table, the muse appeared to be pleased with my handiwork. I flashed her the thumbs-up with a proud grin. *I did this.*

The music eventually slowed down and Lilith got a slow dance. From my new spot holding up the wall, I prayed she didn't get herself into trouble. Her hands were wrapped around his waist as if she was a black widow trying to keep her lover/next meal close. She was facing me with his back turned away. There was a blissful expression on her face. Not exactly one a woman would have when she was content, though. Her eyes formed slits and her hands—not exactly claws—stretched down his back. Michael continued to sway to the music, unaware of how close he was to death in heels.

Eventually, I looked away. Thirst pecked at me, reminding me how long it had been since I'd had a drink. Liquor processed far faster in me than most creatures. If I didn't keep up the fluids I shriveled up like an old raisin in the sun. I darted to the table where my full pitcher was waiting.

The muse was busy typing—probably a love note to an author—on her smart phone, unaware of the guzzle action I had going on with the pitcher. Damn, it was refreshing. From a few tables away, I heard some dudes say, "Even my Uncle Chuck can't put down that much. That's my kind of woman!"

I wish it was beer. Maybe then I could feel a buzz.

Abby looked up. "Where's Lilith?"

"She's slow dancing," I said after a healthy burp. "Probably feeling him up right about now." I made grinding motions with my hips. "She might even get some digits tonight, too."

"Then where are they?" Her normally soft voice darkened.

I twisted around. "They were right there—" I pointed to a spot on the dance floor where a couple was doing their thing. Not a succubus/human one.

"Oh, fuck," I groaned.

"You search the dance floor," Abby said. "I'll check outside to see if they went to get some fresh air."

I combed over the dance floor, even managing to avoid joining some hot guys, but didn't see Lilith or Michael. Lilith's sweet, yet slightly tangy scent lingered where they'd last danced, but it was gone now. Faintly as if they'd been there at least ten minutes ago. I followed the trail. It got cold near the door, though. Too many people going in and out. Panic fought with common sense. There was no way she'd go back on her promise. She told me she'd be good. That she wouldn't ruin a perfectly good night. But as I glanced into the ladies bathroom, only finding humans, and then an empty men's room, a sinking feeling stabbed into my gut and twisted viciously.

A part of me felt really bad. I'd convinced Michael to do this.

I finally made it outside to find Abby. She came up 2nd Avenue, her face reflecting frustration. "I didn't see them."

"Me neither," I admitted. "The trail got cold at the front door."

"So where could they be?" Abby asked.

Standing on the sidewalk, with heat rising from concrete, we glanced around as humans milled about around us, almost expecting Lilith to show up with her arm around Michael's. We'd feel foolish and she'd get a good joke at our expense.

Abby looked down. Then up. "The roof."

"No way." I backed up toward the street until I caught a brief flash of brown hair. It darted out of sight, then reappeared again. "What the fuck is she doing up there?"

"I don't want to know."

I stormed down the sidewalk toward the nearest alley. Abby wasn't far behind. From there, I spotted the closest fire escape. With a quick jump, I made it to the lowest rung and yanked down the stairs. From there, the two of us rushed up to the roof. With each step, I hoped that damn succubus hadn't messed up. Hadn't sucked that poor man dry.

Abby and I had to cross over two buildings, but I didn't need to get up close to see them. There she was, slow dancing with Michael, his back presented to us. Gusts of wind ruffled his curly brown hair. They swayed to the bass from the music below us.

Michael was limp in her arms like a fucking deflated balloon.

I stopped cold. Abby stumbled at my side.

"What the hell did you do?" I moaned.

Lilith's head snapped up, her face filled with guilt. "Just dancing with him."

"D-dancing?" I stuttered. I ran over and snatched him from her arms. Reluctantly, she let go. She didn't reach for him while I searched for a pulse. Rather difficult when the poor guy, who was most likely around one hundred and eighty pounds, wasn't holding up his own weight. Lilith skulked away, whispering softly, "He was so sweet. I just wanted one taste. A sliver of his essence."

"A sliver?" I lifted his arm and it flopped back down. "You were slurping from the bottle a little too much here."

Abby crossed her arms. "I'm really disappointed in you, Lilith."

"I know," she said. "It was really dumb of me."

I exchanged a glance with Abby. Here I was holding this man, his chest hardly moving, and the guilty party hiding her face.

"What do we do now?" Abby asked.

"We can't just leave him on the roof. It will be hot tomorrow and he's not in good shape."

"A hospital?" Lilith suggested.

I glared at her. "I'd love to know how we wheel him into the emergency room. How we explain his *condition?*"

"I think we need a need to make a pit stop to see a wizard," Abby said.

I shook my head. This was gonna suck. Among the supernatural creatures lurking the world, spellcasters like wizards used white magic to heal and help the less fortunate. We all knew one wizard in particular from our therapy group. "Nick is so gonna chew me out for this one."

CHAPTER 3

I've experienced hardship before. Especially when I lived in the sea. Dark things lurked in the ocean's depths. Creatures that hid from the bright lights of the humans' submersibles. But eventually they did come out to hunt for prey. It always happened. No matter what the merfolk did. It was just in their nature to consume. I didn't have to close my eyes to imagine them coming for me. Slithering toward me.

In hindsight, those monsters didn't give me quite the headache the succubus did. And that was why I forced her ass to hold Michael's shoulders while we carried him down the emergency stairwell. The metal moaned with each step we made. Enough to make me question if the structure could hold our weight.

"Maybe we should call Nick," Abby suggested from the alley where she waited for us to come down.

"And ruin the surprise?" I snorted.

My muscles twitched as we reached the ground. He hadn't gotten any lighter. Suddenly, Michael's right arm jerked. The succubus, ever diligent with his care, dropped him. His head hit the concrete with a dull thud.

"Pull yourself together!" I snapped. "Just go get us a cab! Quickly!"

Lilith left us and Abby took her place. "He's okay. Just unconscious."

"As if that's an improvement?" I glanced around. A dumpster blocked the view from the street. "I need your help to hoist him over my shoulder so we can get him into the cab."

"You know, Lilith is probably sorry," Abby said. "You shouldn't be so hard on her."

"I know," I grumbled. With a mighty heave, the muse hoisted Michael over my shoulder. My eyes bugged out and my back spasmed from the weight. The merfolk was pretty strong, but not as strong as werewolves. This dude was over and above my limit. Poseidon's balls, the succubus was gonna owe me big time. I shuffled toward the street with Abby trying to do what she could before the public saw us.

Thankfully, by the time I made it to the curb, just a few pedestrians gave me a weird look. For good measure I muttered, "This is the last time I carry your boyfriend's drunk ass home."

The cabbie, an older Indian man, tried to offer a hand, but Lilith shooed him away. Getting him into the back wasn't pretty. He kind of plopped into the seat—but with some maneuvering of limbs, we got him inside.

Once the door was shut, I gave Nick's address in Brooklyn. If he wasn't home we were screwed.

∿

After a fifteen minute cab ride, we pulled up to rows of brownstones in Brooklyn. As one of Nick's good friends, I'd been here numerous times. Only on the outside, though. Nick never let anyone inside.

Since it was past midnight, the sky was still dark and the only light came from light posts peeking through trees. I dreaded the thought of knocking on his door, but I had no choice.

"Wait while I go see if he's home," I said to the others.

The sidewalk up to his place was quiet. No teens or neighbors walking around. Nobody bothered me as I opened the door and headed for Nick's apartment on the first floor. Before I touched the knocker, I hesitated. Random thoughts of what I'd say went through my head: *"Hey, Nick. Gawd, I fucked up and need help!"*

"You got a great body. Want to see my body...I have in the car?"

"Yo, Nick! We were out partying and we're getting some coffee. Wanna join us?"

I settled for the last response—it had sanity written all over it.

It took a little while for someone to answer the door after I knocked on it, but eventually it creaked open. A slice of light stabbed the darkened hallway and I looked up to see a pale man dressed in black. Even this late at night, Nick had on what he always wore to group therapy: a black trench coat and shiny black shoes. With black hair and dark eyes, he projected a goth-vibe, but when he spoke a quiet serenity flowed through his voice.

"Heidi?" His smile showed his skepticism was front and center. "What are you doing here?"

My mouth dropped open and whatever I'd planned to tell him got sucked away like Michael's essence down

Lilith's throat. My gaze darted into his home and he angled himself to block my view. One peek and I knew why he didn't let anyone inside. Beyond the doorway, all I could see was junk. I'd be the first to admit I wasn't the cleanest roommate. I dropped shit and left it where it fell most of the time. But there was so much my brain couldn't wrap around how someone could live like that. My single glimpse had seared the room into my mind: wands, teapots, a desk covered in papers, an overflowing coat rack. Hardly any place to stand. During therapy, Nick had admitted he had trouble throwing things away, but he'd never said he *literally* didn't toss stuff. That he was a hoarder. I shrugged. We all had things we dealt with.

"Umm, we're having a girls night out and w-we wanted to know if you wanted to come hang out?" Wasn't there something else I was supposed to say? Something about coffee?

Nick slipped out into the hallway and shut the door behind him. "What's this really about? One, you rarely stutter. Two, guys like me don't do ladies night out."

I sighed and gestured for him to follow me. We made our way back to the cab waiting outside. Abby propped up Michael. The muse acted as a barrier between the forlorn succubus and her unconscious date.

Each step I took toward the cab was painful. Especially with the rainbow of emotions that crossed Nick's face: curiosity, surprise, anger, and then disappointment. He reached into the cab, touched Michael's forehead, and then turned to me. "What's going on here?"

Abby and I looked at Lilith.

"I'm sorry!" she squeaked. "Can you just get in the cab or what?"

Nick shook his head while he got into the backseat next

to Michael. The poor man's head flopped forward. Before his upper body followed, Nick used his arm to push him back. The white wizard flashed me a look: *Damn it, Heidi.*

I slid into the front seat, telling the driver to head to the nearest late-night diner, a place off Nassau Avenue where we could figure things out.

Fifteen minutes later, we all sat in an over-sized booth. Michael, with a blank expression on his face, mouth open wide, was leaning on Nick, while the rest of us picked at our food. The temptation to toss one of my tiny square-shaped hash browns into his mouth was strong.

I wasn't surprised Nick didn't want to eat. He was too busy healing Michael. Based on the stupor the human was in, it could be a while.

"How about you three tell me what's going on," Nick said.

Abby told him about the bet. I talked about the club, and finally, Lilith admitted she fucked up and hurt Michael.

"He even said he'd keep my phone number, too," Lilith added sadly.

"Thank goodness you two checked on her. If you hadn't, he'd be dead right now," Nick said firmly. "You need to control yourself, Lilith. No matter where you are." Nick was often one of the therapy group members she tried to cop a feel on.

We finished our meals and made a bit of small talk. Rather hard with the situation at hand.

"This is going to take a while. You ladies head on home." Nick eyed Lilith. "Straight home."

We all nodded. We'd gotten into enough trouble for the evening.

"You two go ahead. I'll pay for the bill," I said to them.

Abby and Lilith headed out while I fished some bills out

of my pocket. I stole a glance at Michael and noticed his face was less pale. A good sign.

"Heidi?" Nick asked.

I glanced up. "Hmmm?"

Nick was quiet for a bit. Almost lost in his own thoughts.

"You didn't see anything, did you?" he asked with a twinkle in his eyes. "Back at my place?"

I grinned. He was my friend and I owed him one. "Nope." I took a final swig of water and left. With the bill paid and Nick minding Michael, I joined the others on the street corner.

"That was quite a night," I mumbled.

"Not the kind I wanted," Lilith said. "I'm so sorry."

"At least you got a date out of it," I said.

"That wasn't date!" Abby said with a snort. "I'm headed home now before you get the idea in your head that you won. C'mon, Lilith."

"Yes, it was," I called to her as they retreated. "It had a kiss *and* a dance. I even saw her feel on his butt."

"Was that before or after she nibbled on him?"

"Oh, those are the smaller details. Don't think about those."

"You *lost*, Heidi," she yelled.

I grumbled a curse.

"See you on the beach tomorrow morning," she called from down the street.

The End

ROCK-A-BYE BABY SUCCUBUS

*Reader's Note: This story takes place after Compelled
(Coveted #3).*

SEXY LADY TIP NUMBER ONE: Once an hour dab a hint of
lipstick on your upper lip to make yourself feel like a billion
bucks. I puckered my lips and smiled at the mirror.
Whoops, I got some lipstick on my teeth.

"Looking foxy, Miss Lilith," I said after I wiped off the
excess lipstick. "Sexy succubus alert."

I love the color red. Red represents sex. Passion.
According to the department store sales lady at Passazh, the
hip shopping mall in downtown St. Petersburg, girls in their
twenties wore this fire engine red color all the time. I made a
clawing motion in the air. *Rawr!* A fireman would have to
put out this *fire.*

A brief painful tug in my lower abdomen made me
grimace.

Almost forgot I was knocked up. I guess a fireman had
already slid down my pole. I giggled and rubbed my

extended belly. Just a few more weeks to go until Yuri's pretty little succubus made her grand appearance.

My hot pink dress Yuri had bought for me sat on our double bed a few feet from our tiny bathroom. We didn't have much in this two-bedroom apartment, but we had love in abundance. A warm feeling coursed over me as I gazed at an ultrasound photo from a month ago. We didn't have long to wait to meet our baby girl.

As I put on my dress, or should I say I wiggled into it with a bunch of grunting, my excitement grew. After much poking and prodding, I managed to manipulate—I mean convince—Yuri we needed a baby shower. According to my mother-in-law, having a celebration before the baby's arrival is considered bad luck. I was an American though and I wanted the experience.

"You need help, *sladkiyaja?*" Yuri yelled out from the living room. He called me *honey* in Russian whenever he thought I needed help. How sweet.

"I got it," I sing-songed with my arms in the air and my dress covering my face. I'd unzipped the damn dress, but the end of the zipper had still gotten caught on my bra. I yanked hard.

Rip!

Well, sex-on-a-stick. I had a hole in the front now, and the zipper in the back was broken too. Nothing I couldn't fix with some safety pins and zebra print duct tape. The last dress got some snazzy stripes that way. A bunch of humans had stared at me, but they were probably jealous of my *keen* fashion sense. A hater is gonna hate. I snagged the duct tape and got to work.

"Are you sure you don't want me to help you?" Yuri called again. "We need to get to the hall before your family gets there."

Ugh, my damn demonic family. Any fun I'd found in taping the back of my dress shut faded at the thought of seeing them. When Yuri's mother had suggested planning everything for me, I got so excited. I mean, who the hell wanted a bunch of attractive incubi and succubi coming to your party and taking all your attention away?

Not that I couldn't hold my own.

I admired my handiwork and slipped on some pearl earrings. Yuri entered the bedroom, and my frown faded away. When he saw me, his eyes brightened.

"What's my *printsessa* doing?" His round form shuffled across the room.

"Getting all dolled up for my prince." I'd spent the past hour applying my makeup. Now I had to do the final touches. Like cramming my sausage-like feet into my boots.

Yuri kneeled in front of me and helped me get them on. I'm so lucky to have found him. I rubbed the shiny spot on his balding head. He had four brown hairs that stubbornly pointed right, but to me he was perfect. My werewolf fiancé had come into my life at a time when I was so lonely. Far too lonely for my kind.

A single phone call from Russia changed my life. During that first international collect call, I had no idea I was talking to the man who'd love me forever. Fifteen hundred dollars in phone bills later, I took a flight to Russia and haven't been back to NYC since. Why go back when I had a good thing here?

"Are you hungry?" he asked with a warm smile.

"I ate last week." It was really two months ago, but technically he didn't need to know that.

My need to drain people of their lifeforce through sex wasn't a subject we often discussed. From the very beginning, Yuri knew my dark nature. He let the matter go—just like he gave into most of my demands: that he have a job, take better care of himself, and stand up like a man. Sitting at home and calling his grandmother back in America for cash wasn't going to help us save up for an apartment of our own. Right now we lived with Yuri's mother Inna.

He kissed the top of my hand. "I do all this traveling with the band so you can eat, but you don't come with me anymore." He touched my belly and the baby shifted. She knew her papa already.

I've almost killed before—just one guy by accident who was so drunk I had to pay someone to check him for alcohol poisoning. In order to feed I traveled with Yuri's folk music band. Keyword *did*. My belly looked like Yuri's now so I didn't feel like watching my man knock out unsuspecting dudes so his fiancée could slurp their souls away.

I sighed. *Had turning into a mother softened me up?*

I hope not. A hot tamale like me still had siren written all over her.

Twenty minutes later, we got to the hall. The place my mother-in-law had picked in south St. Petersburg was fabulous. Russia had such a classic architectural style I loved compared to New York.

Some walls in the small room had water damage spots here and there, but the wallpaper was a lovely yellow brocade. My adopted werewolf family had placed bright pink streamers on the walls and the five tables in the center of the room had lavender-colored lily centerpieces. As expected our family had beaten us here and nearly everyone beamed to see I'd arrived.

Except for three people who continued to sit at a table in the back. One man, dressed in a freshly pressed Armani suit, and two women in designer dresses glanced my way with indifference. My heart dropped.

There went admiring the room.

I told Yuri not to invite *anyone* from my family, but he'd gone over my head—like any good husband—and he'd unknowingly had invited three powerful sex demons to my baby shower.

CHAPTER 2

Before I found Yuri I'd lived an anxious and lonely life in New York City. From one day to another I worked a high-paying job most folks wished they had, and yet, no one wanted me.

Three of the reasons I couldn't find prey in NYC stood before me. After I'd said hello to everyone, Inna had taken my hand and dragged me over there to greet them. Apparently, I had to be nice to the ones who'd left expensive gifts on the table near the far wall.

In broken English she hissed, "I shook big box and it sound expensive."

If I hadn't approached my family, I might've made it through this afternoon without worrying about them. Before my brother spoke, I stood there for a bit.

"Looks like you got in the family way, little sister," Nathaniel said first. "You're a rare one, just like mother." No hellos. As the eldest child of quintuplets, by eight minutes, Nate was considered the golden child among us. He was intelligent, witty, and able to charm the skirt off any woman, but he was also an asshole with no filter.

I will admit though that what he said is true. Nine out of ten succubi don't reproduce. We used the semen of men we drained to impregnate female humans. (Quite gross I know...) Like our mother, I had been born with a human's womb.

I placed an outstretched hand on my stomach as if the baby might hear her asshole uncle. "You're damn right I'm in the family way. My man did it."

My peroxide blonde little sister, who was born three minutes after me, guffawed. I hadn't seen Cristina in so long. She filled her blue Alexander McQueen dress in all the right places. Her light hazel eyes blinked at me with deceptive innocence and her rouged lips slipped into a confident grin. "You call that meal a *man*?"

She continued. "I hope you don't think we're here to celebrate..." Cristina slid her sharp words deeper into me. "Isabeau and I didn't want to come until Nathaniel mentioned how well we'd eat in Russia."

My older sister Isabeau looked me up and down. She was a doppelgänger of our dark-haired mother. At least the spitting image of Mother before she'd been forced into hiding after seducing a witch's philandering husband. "If you can find food to eat looking like that, this place must be a buffet," she said.

"Or a land full of blind people," Cristina added.

"Looking like what?" My fists clenched and my side began to ache. Walking away seemed wise, but I'd done that too many times before. "I've hunted and they can all see me thank you very much." I waved to them. "Now that I've said hello, asshole number one, as well as mean bitch one and two can skedaddle on down the street."

Without an afterthought, I left them behind.

Just like I did when I left America.

THE CHOCOLATE CAKE, which had no decoration other than a layer of frosting, was brick-hard, and the dark-purple punch had a weird smell with hints of black licorice. But, other than that, the party was going well.

I ignored my family, by the way.

Smiling was easy for me now that Yuri took over things. When my fork didn't go through my serving of cake, Yuri hacked off a bite-size piece. Underneath all that fat, my man is all-muscle.

When I kept sipping the punch, but not really drinking the ghastly stuff, Yuri fetched me a drink of water.

After we enjoyed the food, Inna walked up to me. "Time is up and everyone happy. Why don't we take gifts home and open there?"

I nodded, but my first thought had been about the baby showers I'd attended in the US. I'd only been to a few for my human co-workers, but in NYC they'd been lavish affairs in Manhattan. Didn't anyone want to wrap my stomach with toilet paper to guess the number of strips, or watch me make obnoxious cooing noises while I admired my baby's clothes?

Inna offered me a brief hug. "I make Yuri put gifts in car. You sit and wait."

I hid my disappointment. A crowd didn't matter. I had Yuri and that was all that mattered. From the corner of my eye, I saw the gift table. What would it hurt if I *accidentally* ripped the wrap off one of them?

While Inna chatted with Yuri, I hurried over to the table, covert style. Not that I could hide with my waddle, but no one said anything to me as I walked up to the table and poked the largest gift. After one look I had an idea as to who'd brought the silver brocade-covered present: one of my siblings. Cristina drained the lifeforce out of enough sugar daddies to finance fifty baby showers.

The present's folded edges were easy to find so I hurriedly peeled back a portion to reveal a box top. Once I got the top off, I had to bite back the lump in the middle of my throat. The box was filled with precious hand-made baby clothes from an exclusive boutique in East Village. The delicate lace and smooth cotton screamed hand-stitched work. Had Cristina or Isabeau personally picked these out?

At the bottom of the box, I found a note: *custom baby clothes picked by sales rep Mindy at Helena's Boutique.*

I sighed.

Shouldn't I have known better? We are sex demons…

On to the next present. This one was heavy. Inna was coming my way. I had to move faster. I heaved the present up so I could search for a spot to unwrap the gift, but a strange tug in my belly made me pause. A tug and the gush of my water breaking.

My poor Yuri flipped out the moment he saw the blackish fluid on the floor. That little demonic detail wasn't in *What to Expect When You're Expecting.*

The werewolves swarmed me.

"Now?" Inna asked. Maybe she wasn't sure what to say in English.

I'm sure you guessed my American family hadn't moved an inch.

My adopted family forced me to take a seat and hovered over me. One of Inna's in-laws looked me over and nodded with a knowing expression. "The baby has to come out now. No doubt about that."

Well, duh.

A bunch of questions in Russian flew at me, but they spoke too fast for me to catch anything. I was perfectly fine actually, until a stabbing pain forced me to bend over. Yuri took my hand and kissed it over and over again. The gesture was sweet, but futile. Without a demon doula to feed off my pain, this birth would be hell. Pun not intended.

I'd made arrangements for the best demon doula in London. She was scheduled to arrive two weeks from now.

"I go get doctor," Inna said firmly.

I gave Yuri the *don't-you-dare-unless-you-want-to-die* look. Werewolf physicians were glorified veterinarians. My baby was half-werewolf, but I for damn sure wasn't spitting out pups here.

One of the hall staff members ushered us to a private room and I sat down on a sofa. As I lay down, Inna pleaded for us to go to the private doctor most of the werewolves used, but I declined.

What mattered most was my Yuri was with me. Right

now I was crushing his hand, but he grimaced and endured it for me. Another wave of pain faulted across my stomach and I was forced to curl up.

"I'm right here, *printsessa*," Yuri said between clenched teeth.

I was ready to turn his hand into broken bits when a warm palm touched my back and the pain eased a bit. Who was touching me? They smelled sweet. It was one of my sisters.

"Isabeau..." I whispered. "What are you—"

"Just hush."

"What about the others? Won't they mock you for doing this?"

"It doesn't matter." She drew in a deep breath. "Nate and I came to an understanding. While I came in here, he took Cristina out for a meal."

"Why did he do that?" More pain forced me to pause.

"She wouldn't understand why we're doing this. She's still young."

She's younger than me by five minutes... How the hell does that make a difference?

We were quiet for a while. Yuri had left my side to get me a drink. I finally broke the silence. "What epiphany did you have?"

She bit her lip as if her moment of clarity had been hard to find. "I've seen you at your worst, Lilith. Look at you. Your dress is hideous and taped shut. Your shoes are two sizes too big. And your hair! I don't know whether you woke up like that or if you styled it that way on purpose. You are so sickeningly *confident*, and every time we look at you we're ashamed you're a demon like us."

Wow. "Well, fuck, Isa, don't hold back how you *really* feel."

"I'm not done yet." She turned to look at Yuri as he hurried back into the room, his arms overflowing with towels. "With all your imperfections, you have more light and love in your life than any of us will ever have. Our beauty is an illusion, but what you have with Yuri is real."

I tried not to cry right then and there, but it didn't stop the tears that flowed. Having all my siblings here would've painted the perfect picture, but having one was enough.

Over the next three hours, my older sister held my hand and comforted me until the baby arrived. The crowd of Lasovskaya werewolves waiting outside the room tried to hurry in the moment my baby gave her first cry. I couldn't see much with the werewolf ladies crowding me and trying to clean me up. The whole process hadn't been so bad. I couldn't wait to do it again. In a hospital though.

"How is she?" I kept asking.

One lady looked to another.

Isabeau had let go of my head and she slumped to the side. Her vibrant black hair had a streak of gray. She still smiled in the baby's direction.

I wasn't smiling though.

"Somebody needs to freakin' answer me," I snapped. "I don't give a damn if you're werewolves or goblins. I'm about to go fifth level demonic here."

My mother-in-law hurriedly placed the baby in a blanket and handed her to Yuri. He drew his nose along his daughter's precious forehead, then stopped as if caught off guard. He still walked to me with a grin.

"Give me Aleksandra." I held out my arms, ready to see my little lady. Yuri gently placed her into my arms. And, oh, all the pain had been worth it! She was so light. Far lighter than what she'd felt like in my stomach. Her smell was perfect, too. Aleksandra hadn't been washed properly, but her scent promised sunshine and happy makeup sessions in the future. I'd be putting all the pink clothes I'd bought to good use.

Yuri motioned for me to look her over.

"Won't she get cold?" I asked.

"No, werewolves stay warm." He wasn't looking me in the eye.

I carefully unswaddled my baby. Her arms seemed so fragile. Her skin was pink. So perfect. And her legs...

I stopped cold when I looked between my baby's legs.

His legs.

Isabeau peered at him. "I thought you were having a girl."

"I did, too," I mumbled. Every ultrasound, okay the two I had at the human hospital to make sure I wasn't carrying multiples showed me a hamburger (girl parts) and not peas and a carrot (boy parts). My baby didn't even have a baby carrot. His manly bits were micro. Not the best way for an incubus to start out, but like me, he'd be perfect in his own way.

"Aleksandra...Aleksandr is *beautiful,*" I said with certainty. "More than that. He's gorgeous."

Isabeau nodded. "If he's as confident as his mother, he'll make a great incubus *and* werewolf."

I kissed my little prince's forehead, certain that I'd never make my child feel inadequate. Aleksandr had been conceived with love and he would be loved forever more.

I'd deal with all the pink clothes I had another day.

The End

CONTENTS MAY HAVE SHIFTED

CHAPTER 1

Reader's Note: This story takes place a few months after
Compelled (Coveted #3)

"Okay, either someone brought a sack lunch straight from hell or our janitor necromancer has a dead minion who followed him to work," I snapped.

I scanned the expansive flea market, moving from one face in the crowd to the next. Not a single one of my four co-workers said a word. Just another early morning at The Bend of the River Flea Market, also known as The Bends to the locals in South Toms River, New Jersey. The human shoppers browsing our wares didn't know about the supernatural world or the mystical objects that were sold on these shelves.

"It doesn't smell that bad, Natalya," a blonde next to me said.

I threw Erica Holden a raised eyebrow. As a werewolf like me, her nose worked just as well as mine did. Maybe the cloud of designer perfume around her kept the funk at bay, but I could damn well smell it. And it stank to high heaven.

Saturday mornings never fared well for me. At eight-thirty A.M., we had a sizable crowd hungry to rifle through the latest shipments to The Bends. My boss Bill should've been here complaining about the stench and ordering us to handle it. Naturally, the goblin was nowhere to be seen.

Looks like I got to have all the fun. As usual.

Since I couldn't trust the cleanliness habits of my fellow employees, I followed the one thing I could: my nose, which led me through a set of wooden doors into the business office.

If I found one of the janitor's zombie minions shuffling around the desks, he wasn't going to get an invite to the company picnic this year.

The back office was empty. No Bill either.

Maybe my boss was hiding somewhere. Didn't matter, I was on the hunt. Everything in the office was as I'd left it after the workday ended yesterday. The stack of invoices was in a perfect pile, the chairs arranged perfectly behind the desks. Even the merchandise we needed to prep for sale stood at attention.

Except for the old beige steamer trunk on the floor.

Other than the foul stench emanating from it, the faded trunk was a thing of beauty with polished brass hinges and intricate clamps. The edges were slightly marred from where perhaps a dockworker from the past had knocked it about. Under the fog of death, the saltiness of the sea still lingered.

I circled the luggage, noticing strange carvings along the back. They were so tiny the human eye would've assumed they were scratches and nicks. Nothing else seemed amiss.

Until that sucker shifted to the right. I peered over the

side to look at the front again. Something poked out. A large finger, with a sharp talon and black and blue spots mottling the skin, tore a fist-sized hole through the leather near the seam. A four-fingered hand emerged.

What in the hell?

The necrotic fingers flexed along the edge, perhaps attempting to create a bigger hole. My nose twitched from the horrific scent. I hadn't smelled anything that bad since my aunt Vera tossed out six-month-old cabbage that somehow hid in the back of her basement refrigerator.

I took a step back.

Another set of fingers crept through the gap the first hand had formed. Now I had two escapees. The first hand snaked out of the hole, revealing a long gray arm, the skin flaky and scaly. Together, they reached about until one of the hands found the lock along the front.

Then the trunk shook with a hard thump.

A third hand came out to join the first two. Were they attached to one body, or did I have multiple foes to face?

Hell to the no.

With a gentle push—this stuff wasn't mine—I tipped over the trunk onto its side.

"Get back in there!" I grunted.

Another thump from inside the trunk knocked me on my ass. The concrete floor in this room wasn't forgiving.

The trunk jerked to the left on the floor. I plucked the fire extinguisher off the far wall, ready to kick some ass.

Now, to be honest, this wasn't the first magical mishap to go down at The Bends. Most problems though came from backfiring fairy wands to jock-itch-inducing jewelry.

Cruise trunks containing monsters trying to break out was madness at a whole new level. Poised over the gray arm, ready to knock that puppy back in, I bent back to do the yo-heave-ho when the customer service bell rang.

Under most circumstances—pretty much all of them—I scrambled like a werewolf caught butt-naked in human-form at dawn.

Today, I had no choice but to ignore it. Damn it all to hell, I wasn't the only warm-body working here.

Mid-swing that annoying shrill filled the air again.

Anxiety shot up my spine and smacked the back of my head.

Ignore it, Nat.

I hit the arm hard with the fire extinguisher, and the luggage jumped. The second hand swung at me, hard and fast, but I dodged with a jump to the right. My shift to the right pushed me toward the third hand, which slammed me against the wall. Office supplies on shelving rained down on me. More work for me to do, huh?

A growl formed in my chest. The wolf within urged me into a full-out fight. No more obsessive-compulsive tendencies for the day. No more high heels. To hell with my clean blouse and pencil skirt. I advanced on the trunk, grabbing the fire extinguisher on the way.

The shrill ring of the buzzer entered my haze.

Don't answer it. Time to get medieval on the monster in the box.

Buzz. Buzz. Buzz.

I stormed out of the back office, fire extinguisher in hand, ready to knock out whoever thought it was fun idea to do an Irish Line Dance on the button, only to find a group of gaping nuns and a wide-eyed Erica.

"Oh, Jesus," I whispered. I hid what I held behind my back.

"Indeed, Miss Stravinsky," one sister, the shortest, chirped.

Erica plastered her charm on high with her debutante grin. "The Sisters of Divine Grace wanted the antique cross that came in two weeks ago."

Ugh. If there was a hell for goblins, Bill had a first-class ticket. That antique cross was actually a broken T-shaped torture device from the Spanish Inquisition. "And?" I managed. The need to be polite was pivotal here. If you crossed the "SDG," as they were known in South Toms River, their gang-like mentality would mean ruin and dirty looks during the Christmas season.

"We'd like the cross loaded into our truck please," the woman said, her smile crisp and unwelcoming.

"Of course—" A loud crash from the back office made everyone look with concern behind me, but I didn't miss a beat. "—we'll have a staff member load it up for you once we process payment."

The sound of glass breaking forced my jaw shut so tight the back of my teeth sang. "Will that be cash, check, or charge?"

"Is there a problem?" one of the nuns asked. Fear blossomed in the sweat of the tallest one who peered at me with suspicion.

One of the clerks, a fire witch who was checking out customers at the registers, gave me the look. The should-I-stop-what-I'm-doing-and-make-a run-for-it look? I wouldn't be hearing a *Braveheart* rallying cry from her anytime soon.

"I need to see about a trunk," I said as I backed away. "Ms. Holden will assist you with payment while I make sure our staff prepares your cross. It will be a lovely addition to Sunday Mass, I'm sure."

The moment the sisters turned around, I hightailed it to the back office. What was left of it.

One desk was toppled to its side, the supplies on top scattered across the floor. The new panes of glass we planned to use to replace a broken display case window had been shattered to glittery bits. And finally the coup de grâce, that stinky escapee had smashed the box of week-old donuts Bill had left out for his employees. The painfully dry strawberry jelly donuts had bled their gooey centers all over the place like fallen victims.

There was no trunk, but a disgusting trail of grayish goo went from the center of the room to the busted-out double dock doors.

Cinnamon, the telltale sign of spellcaster magic, briefly passed through my nostrils as I got closer to where the trunk had sat. Fear pulsed through me. Something magical had left this place.

From behind me, the doors to the main floor opened.

"So Nat—" Erica stopped cold. "What happened here?"

I pointed toward what was left of the dock doors. "I think our merchandise just made a run for it."

AFTER FIVE HUNDRED DOLLARS' worth of haunted merchandise slithered away, the morning didn't go as well.

"We need to close the store and go after it," I said.

"We should wait for Bill," Erica said firmly. All the while, the expression on her face was stern, but her blue-green-eyed gaze was planted to the ground. I snuck a quick glance at her. She was perfect in so many ways. Compared to my dark brown hair, her blonde curls shined like she was in a shampoo commercial with flawless lighting. Even with a back straightened in frustration and her head turned away from mine, she was still painfully pretty. After nearly six months, I had to remind myself we fought on a starry New Year's Eve night for the ranking of alpha female and I was the one who had won. I was the one who'd snatched her dreams away. All her aspirations for an arranged marriage with the love of my life, Thorn Grantham, came to an end when I won the right to lead the pack.

The topic of he-who-shall-not-be-named, never came up during her training as assistant manager, nor as we worked day-to-day together. It was simple in my opinion: Erica loved power and that power came with the position of alpha female. If she truly loved him, nothing I would've done that night would've come between them. As a werewolf who barely scratched her back the right way, I made a horrible alpha female and my leadership skills were quite lacking.

Which made moments like this one a bit awkward.

"We can't let whatever escaped the trunk to roam the countryside." I took a step toward her. "If that thing is recorded on someone's phone or the public catches wind of it, we're gonna have a lot more than Bill rubbing our fur the wrong way. When magical problems arise in New York City, the magical community sends warlocks to take out the trash." I drove my point home. "Would you like to know what warlocks do to people like us? Would you like to know how they use us for their dark magic?"

Erica stiffened. Her mouth briefly opened, but she sealed her lips just as quickly.

"Would you like a bunch of spellcasters sniffing our butts?" I asked again.

Erica didn't dare look me in the face, but her crossed arms and stiff upper lip told me she didn't want to be involved in matters involving the magical world.

"Unlike you," she bit out, "I'm not equipped to handle this. I'm not a werewolf spellcaster."

So there it was.

Werewolves didn't do magic. According to the Code, or the rules governing werewolf behavior, we didn't dally in magic like witches, warlocks, and wizards. There was a reason for this though, and I had disobeyed such rules to save my mate's life.

"You must think I'm tossing around magic like it's nobody's business." I held in a laugh. "It doesn't work like that, sweetheart. Spellcasting requires a currency I'm not willing to pay." Nor would I ever pay it if I wanted to stay with my husband. "So you and I are going outside and somehow, someway, we're dragging that thing back in here and putting a for sale sign on it."

Her jaw twitched. "Fine."

She went to the overturned desk. I almost groaned when she reached inside the drawer for her purse. What good would that do? Then I smiled. Erica plucked a .45 from her expensive beige handbag and placed the gun into an ankle holster on her leg.

So the woman who brought expensive sushi for her lunches was packing heat? How plucky of her. And daring as well. The Code of conduct for werewolves also forbade us from using guns.

She saw my confused expression and blurted, "I have a Prada handbag. You can never be too careful in a neighborhood like this one."

I snorted. "Yeah, we're overrun with tourists with fanny packs and old ladies with antique fetishes. The danger is crazy real."

Except with that thing out there, it actually was.

Instead of closing the store, I put the college student in charge and not the chain-smoking fire witch who set the counter on fire a few months ago.

Erica and I left through the new gap in the dock doors toward the parking lot. The overcast sky threatened to bring rain and make our hunt even more somber. Thank goodness, there weren't any shoppers in our outdoor area. During this time of the year, we sold more merchandise on the rows of tables out here.

"If you can't do magic, how do you plan to defend yourself?" Erica asked me.

"My *gun* is in my car. I can't take mine to work." I didn't carry a gun per se, but rather a magical weapon I'd acquired during my adventures over the past year.

On the way to my Nissan Altima, I caught a faint whiff of copper. My gaze scanned our surroundings. There wasn't much to see. South Toms River was basically a small town.

The strong, metallic scent of human blood drew us to the edge of the parking lot between The Bends and the next flea market next door.

We found a pool of blood and nothing more next to a beat up, black pick-up truck.

"It's human blood," Erica remarked.

"It's fresh, too."

She glanced at the busy four-lane road not far from us. The trail we needed to follow was was clear. Whatever we were after had headed straight into town.

"Looks like it's had its first meal. Would you like to go back and wait for Bill?" I gestured in the direction we came from.

She ignored me and broke out into a run down the Garden State Parkway.

CHAPTER 3

By the time I fetched my weapon, a handy magical blade, from the back of my car, the mid-morning sunlight was nearly gone. Dampness filled the air and signs of an oncoming rain shower increased with each southward step we took. The thick humidity made the hunt all the more miserable.

No more than twenty feet away to our left, cars zipped past us on two lanes heading southbound on the Parkway. Clusters of trees gave us cover, but they also offered hiding spots for our prey.

Not surprisingly, Erica took point. I was the better tracker between the two of us, but I let her lead for now. Fighting over who'd be attacked first was a waste of time.

The goblin blade hummed in my hand. Usually as active as a fork sitting on the dinner table, the goblin blade twitched now. Almost as if it sensed something supernatural lurking nearby. The weird weapon ended up in my possession during a trip to save my dad from the werewolf Russian mafia in Atlantic City. While cornering a conniving goblin bent on capturing my mate and me, I happened to take the little, silver blade he tried to cut me with—not knowing that the goblin blade transformed into a new weapon based on the nearest supernatural threat to the owner's proximity. All the attempts I made to return the goblin's toy failed.

I guess it was mine for now.

The trail took us southwest past the subdivisions. Past the little league fields and playgrounds with perfectly good morsels of humans to eat. Then the houses disappeared and our path became all too familiar once we crossed Double Trouble Road and came to a stop in front of a long driveway.

"This place looks familiar," Erica murmured.

"Yeah, it would be because it's my old house."

Before I'd fought Erica and moved in with Thorn at his house on the other side of town, I'd lived here alone as the pariah of the South Toms River Pack.

I had all sorts of memories here—most of them good—but right now unease tickled the back of my neck. Normally, the forest surrounding my two-story cottage offered a wall of protection from the judgmental outside world, but with that creature potentially stalking my hallways, I felt thrown off a bit.

"Any idea why it came here?" A hint of suspicion lined Erica's words.

"You have to be kidding me." My sigh was heavy with sarcasm. "I dunno. Especially since the last crazed monster meeting I held was at my mom's house."

Erica rolled her eyes. After she pulled her gun from her ankle holster, she hurried down the driveway, and I followed. As we approached the house, the shadows along the trees grew ten-fold. The cottage, with its bright red shutters and whitewashed wood, seemed more like an evil witch's hideout from a fairytale than a regular home.

I scanned my surroundings from the tree line to the house's roof. Branches swayed about with a growing wind. Wildlife that roamed during the day had already sought shelter. While I checked for danger, I tried to push away the obvious.

Erica had a right to be suspicious. Something weird had showed up at The Bends, and while it could have gone anywhere, it went straight to my former house. Not the place where I currently resided, but a place I used to live. Had an old enemy of mine sent me a gift? After everything that had happened over the past year, the likelihood that I had a cushy spot on someone's Shit List was quite high.

As we got closer to the house, the knife's hilt grew warmer. My heartbeat sped up. With each step, anxiety bled into my senses, making it harder for me to focus on what I had to do.

"You all right, Natalya?" Erica glanced at me.

My face grew warm with embarrassment as I nodded. Hiding fear among fellow pack members was near impossible. The wolf within me whined, but I didn't so much as speak. I came here to handle business and I planned to do it. I tossed to her the keys to the door.

Erica fumbled with the lock then paused. Her head tilted to the right. Did she hear something I couldn't?

Then I heard it. A faint scratching above our heads on the porch roof.

The wooden hilt in my hand elongated, extending until the wood became marble and the metal blade darkened from silver to black. The weapon was about my five-foot-eight height. Tiny letters, like the ones I'd seen on the trunk, were carved into the stone.

Not good.

Every time this damn blade transformed I had no idea what I faced. A broad sword or a battle-axe I could handle. But when the goblin blade transformed into a weapon like the one I held, I had no idea what kind of madness I was about to step into.

For all I knew, my lance's strange writing read, *"Run stupid!"*

The scratching sound wasn't far away now. The closest thing I could compare the noise to was fingernails dragging something heavy across the porch roof...

Claws appeared first.

But they were much bigger now.

Erica twisted toward the movement, her gun drawn, but neither of us had time to react before a pungent mass flew between us. With a wet plop, the creature landed on the porch stairs.

My face contorted with disgust.

What I'd seen earlier had been no arm, but the legs of a beast with a serpentine body, a rooster's head, and black, bat-like wings. Its scaly, green torso shined from the stinky, bubbling fluid covering its skin. The creature, now the size of a Great Dane, hissed at us from its hooked orange beak.

"Oh, gross!" Erica shot first and asked questions later.

Bullets pelleted it, but the few that hit didn't keep it from rushing me. My lance went up in time to deflect its attack. The lance's blade stabbed it deep in its midsection. *Gotcha.* It squawked and bounded away, crashing across the porch and through the living room window.

I headed for the front door, but Erica grabbed my arm.

"Are you crazy? We need to call for help against th-th-that thing. Those bullets did nothing."

"That thing is a *basilisk*." Only once in my life had a seen one, and that particular time, I was reading a picture book. Unlike the harpies and other malevolent creatures I'd encountered in person, the basilisk was considered very rare and legendary. As gross as this harbinger of pure evil appeared, I now understood why.

"I don't give a *fuck* if it's a chicken or a snake. It's not natural." Her normally refined composure collapsed as she jerked her gun toward the house. "If we can't get help from those warlocks, then we need the pack. What about the Stravinskys?" She paused briefly. "What about Thorn?"

Did she really just say my husband's name? "He left town this morning on pack business. He's not available, but I could call my family—"

A crash inside the house told me the basilisk was wrecking my place. If it so much as broke a single...*Screw waiting.* I yanked my arm free and kicked down the door.

CHAPTER 4

With the curtains drawn, the inside of my house was dark except for slivers of light reaching across the floors. The living room, where the basilisk had entered, was well-lit yet trashed. The intruder's escape path was evident from the scratches across the wood floor, the gouges it ripped into the couch as it scampered over the furniture, and finally, to the wall where it crashed into my storage boxes filled with fragile collectibles.

Rage built in my stomach when I spotted massive dents in the boxes. "That motherf—"

"Quiet!" Erica picked up a lamp and crept toward the stairwell. The wet path went that way. "We need to sneak up on it somehow."

"Don't you have more bullets?" I hissed.

"I haven't been caught breaking the Code's firearms rule yet, but I'm smart enough to not carry a bunch of extra clips around." Her head whipped in my direction to give me a dark look.

"Then I should take point." Reluctantly she let me go

up the staircase first. A few times on the way up, I had to hold onto the banister. Gooey shit covered everything.

By the time I reached the top of the steps, most of the determination that fed me on the bottom floor disappeared. The stench was overwhelming—practically to the point that I couldn't track my prey by scent.

Where is it?

We crept along the hallway. Two bedroom doors were open. The wet trail ended along both.

So where could it go?

The dead silence ended as we were thrown to the floor from above. That sneaky rooster-chicken-whatever-the-hell it was clung to the ceiling and dropped down on us ninja-style.

I rolled from under it, jumping up to swing the lance around. Only to have it swing into the wall. Could you tell I often used these things?

The basilisk continued to hold a now-growling and snapping Erica against the floor, the claws from its four hands digging into her torso.

I swung the magical lance around—correctly this time—and repeatedly stabbed that son-of-bitch like my life depended on it. "Get off her!"

The basilisk's squawk turned into an ear-piecing shriek when one of my jabs pierced between its black wings and went deep. It whipped its long tail in my direction, forcing me back.

With a hard twist to the right, Erica slammed the lamp across the bleeding basilisk's head and sent it careening into my old bedroom. It landed on my bed, bleeding from its wounds and oozing disgusting goo all over the place.

I jumped over Erica and rushed it. *Hold tight to the lance, Nat. Time to end this.*

The lance's obsidian blade slid straight through the basilisk's body into the wall, effectually pinning it. For now, anyway. It reached for me, clawing and biting at the pole. The flapping of its wings made it hard to hear anything.

Then it slid forward a bit along the pole, edging closer to me. Its nimble fingers got closer and closer.

"Erica!" I gasped. If I moved back, I'd free it.

She slowly got up, holding her bleeding stomach. Was she hurt badly? With each step she took toward me, her steps grew steadier. "I'm here."

"Pin it," I grunted, jerking my head to the dresser on the other side of the room. Using her shoulder, she shoved the dresser across the floor until it held the basilisk in place.

"I'm moving!" I warned her. I stabbed it again and again. I got in more stabs than the chicken kabobs got at my aunt's house during Stravinsky family barbecues.

The basilisk grew silent. When it finally moved no more, I stumbled away.

"Is it really dead?" Erica asked.

"Good question." I advanced on the carcass, ready to do a few more hits for good measure, but the basilisk melted into a wet puddle. A puddle that stank just as bad as the basilisk did.

"It's gone," I said.

Erica sagged against the dresser.

"Will you be all right?" I approached her to check, but she shied away from me.

"It's just a few scratches." She shrugged, but even I could smell her pain. Her pride would keep her from showing me weakness.

There were so many horrible things she'd done to me in the past—beatings, verbal abuse—but the pain I'd experienced should be her burden and not mine. I let her be and fetched her a towel.

By the time I caught my breath, it took everything I had, including popping a few anti-anxiety pills, to stop myself from *really* looking at the sad state of my former home. I was alive. Erica was alive.

The rest could be dealt with in time.

I opened the bedroom window to air out the room and spotted someone standing outside the house.

Of course, there was our goblin boss. The cavalry had arrived. Conveniently late, I might add. "Holy shit. I hope you got good insurance, Nat."

To humans, Bill was just a tall, thin man with wire-framed glasses. But I'd seen goblins for real, and they were quite ugly and reeked of magic with a bitter tang of iron. The invisibility spell he used was quite welcomed.

"Good insurance?" I snapped. "I bet The Bends has no plans to compensate me for the damages."

Bill was the kind of guy who scrambled for dropped change off the flea market floor. I wasn't getting a damn thing. I took in my bedroom. My bed smelled like shit. My whole house smelled like shit. Which meant there was no way in hell I was sleeping tonight at my new house until every inch of this slimy crap was wiped up.

Effectively pissed now, I began to clean up while my co-worker slowly healed. As I tossed soiled linens out my bedroom window, Bill joined us.

He tsked at the sight. Erica continued to sit against the dresser as if she was glued to it.

"So what are we taking back again?" she murmured. Even her voice sounded tired.

She had a good point there. Most likely the trunk wasn't back at The Bends and the creature was gone now.

"I don't know." I turned to Bill. "Do you know anything about the steamer trunk or the basilisk we found inside?"

He shrugged. "Beats me. I bought it cheap off the goblin market, and someone delivered it."

I sighed. It was always about money. Nothing he'd bought before though had ever attacked us like this. "What about the man who owned the black truck? The man who got eaten."

"Took care of it," Bill replied. "He was a drifter passing through town."

Bill's nonchalant attitude forced a growl from my throat. "How do you know that guy didn't have a family?"

Bill stiffened. "I said I took care of it, Nat. Unless you're willing to cast a spell or two. Perhaps call in a favor?"

"Not happening." He knew very well I'd learned a thing or two, and I wasn't willing to pay the price to do werewolf magic.

"*Some prices are worth paying,*" my grandma Lasovskaya always said. She'd saved my life using werewolf magic, but I'd seen the cost and it wasn't worth it to me. I was going to live as long as possible with Thorn now that we had each other again. No spell was worth losing that.

I paused in the middle of working as my unease grew again. The basilisk had known where I had *lived*.

Someone placed a target on my back.

"So you don't know where it came from or why that thing was hiding in my old house?" I asked.

Bill shrugged and pushed his glasses up his nose. The smile on his seemingly innocent, pale face sent a chill up my spine. "That's the crazy thing about dark magic, Natalya. You might think you've dodged the worse of it, but what goes around seems to always come back around again."

If this was just the beginning of what was coming for me, I was scared senseless of what might come next.

The End

COVETED

Prequel
Novella
0.5

Book
1

Book
2

Novella
2.5

Book
3

Short Story
Collection

Prequel feat.
Aggie
McClure

VALKYRIE
RISING
PRESS

ABOUT THE AUTHOR

Shawntelle Madison is a Web developer who loves to weave words as well as code. She'd be reluctant to admit it, but if pressed, she'd say that she covets and collects source code. After losing her first summer job detasseling corn, Madison performed various jobs, from fast-food clerk to grunt programmer to university webmaster. Writing eccentric characters is her favorite job of all. On any given day when she's not surgically attached to her computer, she can be found watching cheesy horror movies or the latest action-packed anime. Shawntelle Madison lives in Missouri with her husband and children.

www.ingramcontent.com/pod-product-compliance
Lightning Source LLC
Chambersburg PA
CBHW020339180726
47991CB00020B/1764